FEATHERS OF TRUTH

BRITTON BRINKLEY

Feathers of Truth
Britton Brinkley

Landingham Stanley Press

Copyright © 2023 by Britton Brinkley

All rights reserved.

No portion of this book may be reproduced in any form without written permission from the publisher or author, except as permitted by U.S. copyright law.

Author's Note

Feathers of Truth was originally written as part of a paranormal found family anthology, The Blood of the Covenant. It was my first anthology and I'll be honest, I had no idea what to write. I STRUGGLED to get this story on paper at first and didn't like it, but by the time I finished it, I was IN LOVE.

Feathers blurs the lines of what it means to be a good and a bad guy. It takes the urban setting of Chicago (some of it real and some fictional) and turns it into a paranormal playground. I've always loved the idea of a whole other world operating beside us. That's what I tried to create here. A werewolf, or a phoenix, or a warlock could be sitting right beside you on the train or your next-door neighbor. Would you even know it?

Another thing I'd like to point out is, that when I started this story, it was meant to be a standalone, just for the anthology, and that's it. Shocker, it's going to be at least a trilogy, with several spin-offs and connected to at least one other paranormal story coming soon.

Please don't yell at me for the ending! Enjoy!

Trigger/Content Warnings:

- Murder
- Guns
- Assault
- Stalking
- Torture
- Death of a Parent
- Crime Scenes
- Blood
- Explicit Sexual Content
- Explicit Language

FEATHERS OF TRUTH

For the most up-to-date list of content and trigger warnings:

One

That saying "you only live once" applies to the creatures and people walking this earth, but not me. Never me.

A wicked grin pulls at the corners of my full lips. The tiniest gesture that would terrify any normal human, but not the burly one in front of me, with his gut lolling over the waistband of his slacks. Dirt and grime clinging to his fingernails and cheeks. Rivulets of sweat break free of the streaks of gray at his temples down his mottled skin.

On the surface, he looks unimposing. Non-threatening. No one would ever fear this glutinous piece of shit casually walking past them on the street. More likely pity him for the extra weight around his middle and neck, and the sheen that always seems present on his forehead.

They don't know that he runs one of the world's largest drug organizations. His cocaine quality irresistible to druggies of all types. A hit of heaven they'll never get elsewhere. Mario Silarno is one of the most dangerous men to grace our streets, but the man I work for wants him dead. I don't care or know why. All I know is Mr. Silarno made a grave mistake when he pressed the muzzle of his gun against the pristine skin of my forehead.

I can sense the uptick in the rhythm of his pulse. Not from fear. No, this man fears nothing but losing his high-paying clients. It's from the extra exertion of his heart. The adrenaline making the weakened organ work too hard when he found me clad in my favorite leather jacket and skinny jeans, nestled into the armchair in the corner of his study. The gloom of the night slithered through the opening between thick curtains, covering me in shadows while I waited. My hits never know I'm coming... until I'm here.

"What the fuck are you doing in my house?" Spittle flies past his thin lips, streaking my face in the stench of steak and cigars. Dude could use a serious breath mint but never mind that now.

"Oh, Mario. I think you know." The flirtatious lilt to my words a pseudo-security blanket, confusing him. His mind whirring at warp speed, attempting to determine who I work for. Just who has come to take what he built?

I came to take from him, but not what he thinks. He protects his drug empire. I protect the interests of the man behind the curtain. The one who has paid me millions over the years to dispatch the scum — and sometimes good people — he no longer wants to inhabit the Earth. I've never asked questions. I don't care. In the end, the answers won't change anything for me. They won't make me any less alone than I already am.

"Get the fuck out of my house, you bitch."

My smile widens as his face reddens. The anger and irritation surfacing in a torrent of emotion. Many men are like him, living as cavemen, expressing a minimal range of authentic emotions.

We've been alone in this compact room long enough for our eyes to adjust. For him to take in the features of my face. The scrunch of his brow revealing his concentration. Memorization he won't need in the next five minutes.

The high cheekbones. Sultry mouth like Angelina Jolie. Slanted dark eyes and bridged straight nose. On the outside, the appearance of a supermodel, an asset I've used to my advantage my entire life. It's easier to get what you want when you have a gorgeous face and cunning wit to get by in life. Thankfully, my looks serve as a glamor for what I am. A revelation that nearly crippled me with excitement at ten years old.

"What are you going to do with that, Mario?"

My forehead presses into the gun. His arm only recoiling slightly. A slip in his guise of pretending he has complete control over this situation. As if convincing himself he's not experiencing the dread finger-walk its way up his spine, he pushes back. The metal no longer cool against my warm skin. The rim heating to match my rising temperature.

"I. Will. Shoot. You." The punctuation of each word meant to frighten me into submission. Little does this twat of a man know I bow to no one. Not even the one who pays me for the unspeakable deeds I do.

"Pull the trigger. By the time I leave here tonight, you'll be dead and this place will be up in flames."

Mario's Adam's apple bobs in his throat, his audible gulp echoing throughout the enclosed space. *Good*. I Like him shaking in his boots and wondering if my threat is real. It is. He could shoot me countless times, but in the end, he'll be the only one no longer amongst the living.

Slowly, I rise to my feet, the gun firmly still pressed against my skull. To his credit, he doesn't flinch as I move toward him, torturous step by step, his elbow finally forced to bend to accommodate for me closing the distance between us. His breath leaves his parted lips in unsteady pants. No longer able to hide how uncomfortable he is. As if possessed by my intent, his steps mimic my own. The click of my heels forwards the beacon for the draw of his thudding steps back until his thighs meet the side of his mammoth mahogany desk.

"Let's make this easy, shall we? I'm starving and you've wasted too much of my time here."

Boredom bleeds into my words. A clear sign that I've already spent more time here than I'd intended to. The last thing I need is for him to shoot. An even bigger zap on time, requiring my return, and then chasing after his lard ass as he tries to escape from his self-proclaimed palace here.

"You'll put down the gun. Do as I say. Then I'll be out of your hair in no time." My nonchalance punctuated by a careless shrug.

Thick brows knit together. A dead giveaway that he's contemplating doing as I ask.

"What do you want?" Hesitation guiding his question versus the anger at finding me here. Confidence wanes as I continue to stare him down with the muzzle of his gun still against my head.

"Only what my boss wants. So, will you cooperate or will you make this hard for me?"

Another swallow, as the gun shifts in the slightest. Just enough for me to swoop in and trap his wrist under my armpit, twisting and grabbing the gun with my left hand. Yet another way I am unusual. He's panting now, his flabby chest heaving under the white button-down shirt, perspiration soaking through the fabric.

It's my turn to point the gun at his head. He doesn't beg, just stares me down as I pull the trigger. The quiet thunk of the bullet hitting bone before his body slumps against the desk to its resting place — music to my ears.

There's no point in cleaning off my fingerprints. They won't find ones like mine. A smile graces my face as I stroll from the study.

No looking back. Never look back.

With a single ring, my cell connects me to my boss. "It's done." Just as quick a click ends the call. There's nothing else to say.

By all means, murdering Mario Silarno should have been a greater challenge. I was convinced he would pull the trigger. No matter. He could have a million times. Lucky me, nothing kills what I am.

There's no death for the last Phoenix in existence.

Me.

Two

Violent wind whips at my shoulder-length hair, the waves loosening as they swirl and flip through the air. There's no such thing as Fall in Chicago. We go from warm weather to a slight chill, barreling into winds that threaten to carry you away, then dumped into blistering cold. We're teetering on the edge. The threat of snow is right around the corner. It's a quiet night out here in the suburbs of Winnetka. All the wealthy families long since tucked into their beds in their silk pajamas.

The click of my heels and the crash of the waves of Lake Michigan — not far to my right — serve as my soundtrack as I make my way back to my 4Runner. What I like to call my upgraded mommy-and-me van I use when coming into the burbs. It allows me to be inconspicuous. Blend in with all the other moms toting around their toddlers and teens when I come to places like this.

The engine roars as I start the car. Nothing but waving trees around me as I pull out onto the road and head for downtown. The roads are nearly empty at eleven p.m. on a Thursday night. As they should be. The traffic-free trek, not giving me adequate time to fixate on my Phoenix. At its displeasure of remaining caged tonight. There are only ever two occasions when it emerges. With death and when I call, reaching down into the belly of my being where it sleeps, dormant until needed.

I was ten years old when I realized what I was. Back then, I lived in the mountains of Montana with my adoptive family. The loving couple that found me abandoned on the side of the road.

There was a cliff with a deadly drop-off that served as our extended backyard. The very one I was explicitly told to never play near. I've never been one to listen, even from a young age. I went there most days, peering over the edge at the burnt sienna rock leading to the rolling river below. Even then, I knew I could fly. I felt it within me. So one day, I jumped.

I remember the rush of air on my face as my eyes shut. Just a tiny moment of being transported back in time. The pale blue dress I was wearing billowed around me. The cool air sent goosebumps across my exposed flesh. As quick as they came they faded, my skin heating, the sensation so much more intense than any fever I'd ever had. As if a record on repeat, I told myself I could fly. Over and over and over. Waiting for magical wings or fairy dust or something to keep me from becoming the new decor for the rocks and water below.

The fall seemed to be in slow motion as feathers the color of the sun spread across my arms, and writhing flames enveloped them. I cried out, thinking my flesh would burn, but it didn't. Only seconds for my entire body to change from the tall, lanky girl to a creature that only existed in the magical worlds of my books. With a snap, what had been my pouty mouth was a beak. My vision, which was near perfect, enhanced, allowing me to see for miles. My first taste of what power felt like. I loved it.

I was no longer falling, but... floating. My wings — each longer than my five-foot-two frame — stretched to the sides, catching the wind, so I soared over the flowing water instead of crashing into it. I flew there for hours that day, watching my reflection, admiring the creature I became. As a child, I should have been scared, but inside, I was elated. I strove to be different, but this proved I really was. It was a secret only for me.

Over the years, that secret faded from a happy one to one of loneliness and seclusion. By the time I was twenty and making my way through college, I'd become so recluse I doubt anyone would have noticed if I disappeared. That was the year I took up shooting lessons and self-defense. I may have been magic, but I was still a woman, walking around my college campus late at night, attempting to find places to let my Phoenix soar.

It wasn't until I turned twenty-five and moved here to Chicago, becoming a CPD cop that Salvatore Danarius, my boss, found me. Even now, as I slide onto my favorite bar stool, all the way at the end, tucked into the corner, I can feel his essence next to me. An invisible presence reminiscent of the night he found me. I was in this very seat, nursing the same Basil Hayden. Taking small sips to feel the burn on my insides. The only inconspicuous way to feel the way my Firebird made me feel.

After my kills, I come here. Often enough that Mike, the bartender, doesn't even need verbal communication from me to have my glass waiting directly in front of the only stool I ever sit on. Seven years of routine will do that. Me dispatching of men and women that never see me coming. Most know that someday someone will come to take their thrones. I am that someone that arrives in the night. I'm the last set of eyes they look into before they die.

To this day, I don't know why Sal approached me. What he saw in the dark depths of my oddly colored eyes that made him pick me. The number of times I've been told I've never seen a black woman with navy blue eyes is exhausting. I assume it has something to do with my lineage. With what I am. I never knew my biological parents, so there's no way for me to know. Sometimes I wonder if that's why they gave me away. Their soul-crushing reason for not wanting me. I wish I knew if they were dead or alive. I would yank the answers from them before burning them to the ground for leaving me alone in this big, wicked world.

But I've done my research over the years. I am supposed to be a myth. I'm not supposed to exist. Years of countless nights wasted rummaging through old texts for someone like me. Another phoenix to be a kindred spirit with, and I've never found one. Not a single one. Only legends of what I am.

Twirling the glass between my fingers, eyes focused on the glistening amber liquid, I ignore the male body that slides onto the stool next to me until his gravelly voice drags me out of the depths of my thoughts.

"Why does a gorgeous woman like you look so lonely?" The stranger asks, his own glass, full of light beer visible in my peripheral vision.

"Gorgeous people can be lonely too," I scoff, downing the remaining two fingers of my drink. Mike hands me another glass before the original touches the wood of the bar. I down that one too. Three large gulps as the burn glides over the delicate tissues of my throat and belly.

Not bothering to fix the bored expression on my face, I glance at the man next to me. Powerful jaw. Pronounced nose. Doe-brown eyes that sparkle. Complexion battling Casper for the pasty award. Freckles dot majority of his face, neck, and exposed forearms. Thick forearms, corded with muscle. He'll do. Anything to curb the loneliness. Even just for a while.

"My place or yours?" My last words before downing my last bourbon of the night.

His brows raise in surprise. Fumbling hands clasping around his own glass before chugging his beer and wiping his lips with the back of his hand. His heavy footfalls follow me out into the whipping wind of the Chicago night, thick fingers pressing into my lower back.

Time for a little fun.

Three

No surprise he lives just like most single men my age in this city. Minimalistic furniture with just enough class to convince people he's more sophisticated than he actually is. The one small mercy is the lack of nasty gym shorts and crumpled boxers strewn about as I follow him into the cramped corner kitchen. Refusing to turn on the lights, only the soft glow from the open refrigerator door aids me in gawking at the man before me.

He has a stronger frame than I realized on that bar stool. His height towering over mine. A challenge sometimes when you're a woman that's five-ten and wears almost exclusively six-inch heels everywhere you go. He's already removed his coat, the thin shirt straining as it's stretched across the bulging muscles of his back. He's quite the specimen. I hope his dick matches the rest of him or it'll be another night of me faking an orgasm and doing my best to disappear as quickly as possible.

"Hope Sam Adams is okay." He shrugs, handing me the newly opened bottle. I drink deeply, letting the carbonation fizzle down my throat and bloat my belly. Not as good as the fire of the bourbon, but it will do.

Just to be clear, this has nothing to do with liquid courage to screw this guy. No, I have no shame in my sexual promiscuity. I like to fuck. A lot. Doesn't matter who he is. Yet another perk of being what I am, is disease never claims my insides. So, I've never been concerned with contracting anything from my various partners. But still, I abide by the "no glove, no love" rule, mostly.

I don't date. Relationships are something too personal. A bond I'm not willing to engage in; lacking the luxury of giving that person all of me. I can see it now, "Hey handsome. Glad we're getting along so well. Just so we're clear, I'm a Firebird that's reborn if I die. You cool with that?"

"This works." I tip the half-empty bottle in his direction, leaning against the unforgiving edge of the counter. He's staring at me as he takes repeated swigs from his bottle. Nerves. This isn't something he does.

"Show me your room," I smirk. Turning my back to him, I saunter down the narrow hallway to the right. Destination bedroom. Hand outreached, I push the door wide as I enter.

The comforter and pillows draped across the bed are crisp and clean. Everything in its place. The blue light of the television shining bright against the dark. I stare at it, captivated by the color. Since I realized what I am, I've dreamt many nights of a phoenix, just like me, but with feathers of cobalt, bright and vibrant, just like the light glaring at me.

Giant hands snake around my waist as he sidles up behind me, his hard length already pressing into my lower back. Tender lips trail up the side of my neck, heating me in an entirely new way. Spinning in his arms, I tug his head down to me. My fingers tangling in the hair at the nape of his neck. The man can kiss. Let's pray he can fuck, too. Because I need one. A way to bang my sins out of my system. To forget that I just murdered someone else without even blinking.

Clothes shed from our bodies, thrown into various corners of the room, leaving him naked, his rigid cock pressed between our bodies, and me in nothing but my lace bra with the extra lines of fabric cutting across my cleavage. Bending at the waist, he shoves the cup aside, biting my nipple between his teeth, drawing a groan out of me. I like it when it hurts. When they're rough. When they don't question if they could actually damage my not-so-fragile body.

Our feet and legs tangle as I force us to the wall, shifting at the last minute so my back slams into the hard surface. He's surprised by the laugh that escapes me but doesn't hesitate to thrust his tongue back into my mouth and his fingers into my pulsing core. *Fuck.* Those damn sausages he has for fingers fill me more than I would think possible. His stroking and probing against my walls, pulling at the storm brewing in my lower belly.

"Quit dicking around and get to work," I growl, pulling his face back from mine by fisting his hair.

So many women want to be wooed and worshiped. Not this one. I want to be fucked stupid. Ravaged until I forget my name. Forget my past. Forget that I am completely alone in this world. That there's no one like me.

My giant does as he's asked, large hands gripping under my round ass and hauling me into the air without a bit of effort. Before I can pull him close, the telltale ruffle of foil fills the space. His hand sliding between us to sheath himself. Instinctually, my aching thighs wrap around him tighter as he draws back his hand, dragging him close. Hand braced between us, I edge him into my entrance. Thanks to the no sickness thing, I prefer to go bareback when men are willing, but most humans do their part. No babies wanted here.

The one thing I'm unsure of is pregnancy. I've been on birth control since I was a teenager because one thing phoenixes still have is a menstrual cycle once a quarter. So I figured I could still become pregnant just like anyone else. I wasn't having sex back then. Choosing to guard my virginity until after I graduated college. Still, a baby was not something I wanted at all in those days.

Age has softened me, though. The need for me to find that blue phoenix of my dreams lingering in the back of my consciousness. What it would be like to actually share my life with someone? Like my co-workers and their families.

With no concern for my comfort, he thrusts in with a single flex of his hips. Punishing my core for squeezing him tight. The first orgasm rages through me. The fire that lives within roaring beneath my skin with enough ferocity, focused concentration is the only way to keep it locked down. I wouldn't want to fry the guy while we're having such a good time. With steady breaths, my bird relaxes again, riding out the orgasm as our hips grind together, my fingers jamming against my clit to draw it out.

"Fuck. You feel so good, baby."

"Mmmhmm," I hum in response. Nothing I haven't heard before. A line most men use. They love a tight cunt and a willing woman to fall into bed with them. Or in this case, the floor as he trips over some article of our clothing, my back crashing into the carpet.

His rhythm doesn't slow, the pumping of his hips and his wide girth threatening to tear me apart. I need every bit, as my teeth sink into his freckled shoulder. His growl only makes my muscles squeeze him tighter, keeping him from retreating from my slick heat. In an instant, he's thickening inside me, his balls drawing up.

With as much strength as I can muster, I throw him from me. His large body landing in the spot just next to me.

"What the hell?" he groans.

"I'm not done with you yet." My tone, flirtatious.

Let them come, it'll be the only one.

It's too soon. I need at least another three orgasms before I'll be satisfied.

Lying back on the edge of the bed, I spread my legs wide, running my lithe fingers through the arousal now dripping down my inner thighs. "Come clean up this mess."

Like a dog eager for a treat, he crawls to me, eyes never leaving mine. The darkness of the room makes them appear as black as demons. Gripping under my thighs, his thick arms hold me in place, the tip of his tongue driving up through my sensitive flesh.

Not only can the man screw, but he eats pussy like he was born to. Licking, sucking, and biting in the right places. His pace intensifies the pleasure, curling my toes. It's not long before my second release ricochets through me, my abdominal muscles convulsing from the force of it.

The giant gives me four more orgasms before I finally sit up on the edge of his bed, slipping back into my lace panties.

"What the hell is that?" he croaks from behind me. His colossal frame laid out on the opposite side, the thin sheet doing nothing to hide the outline of his thick length.

I know what he's referring to. The tattoo on my back that trails down the underside of both my arms. He wouldn't have seen it because I never had my back to him. The answer is always the same. I give no explanations when they ask.

Refusing to answer just yet, I finish shimmying into my jeans, boots, and t-shirt.

"Well?" he questions.

"It's me," I whisper before disappearing out of the bedroom and quietly shutting the apartment door behind me.

Four

The choice to become a cop had nothing to do with being noble. Not driven by stopping criminals or being outraged because a family member was murdered, the case now cold. An endless collection of evidence accumulating dust in the basement of a police station. It was about the thrill. The danger. Surges of adrenaline to pump through my veins. It was hard to find time and places to let my Phoenix fly free. A constant emptiness inside me being deprived of that high.

I had a friend obsessed with true crime. Her favorite pastime, reciting the ever-changing murder rates across the country. Chicago's had skyrocketed.

That was my sign. Become a cop. Get my thrills from dangerous situations. Per the legends I'd studied for hours as an undergrad, it's near impossible to kill a phoenix. No matter what, I should be reborn. I was banking on that when I became a rookie cop. A fearless woman in a sea of arrogant men, with a compulsion to live on the edge.

Being a street cop was enough for a while, but I wanted to be on murder cases. Making detective was the only natural progression. The position I've been in for the past two years. Working my ass off to be the only female homicide detective in my precinct. It works for me. The guys are crass, but that just means I can be too. But being one of the guys means getting teased like one.

"Hey, Luxe. Rough night?"

No doubt I look as ragged as I feel. I got a good romp in, but it only took the edge off temporarily. I'd sat awake on my balcony all night, sipping more bourbon than I should have. Legally, I'm likely still considered drunk at the moment, but my magical blood also means I recoup quickly. Internally, that is.

Externally, my eyes are likely bloodshot. My waves not styled into submission, but my natural pattern now wind-tossed. I didn't bother putting on makeup this morning. We're lucky my dress slacks and blouse even happened instead of a hoodie and leggings. Mornings like this the mirror is not my friend.

"I could ask you the same, Gomez," I snort back at my partner. His taunts saved just for me. A straight-shooter with more sarcasm than a Brit. It's why we get along.

Other than our complexions and dry humor, there's nothing remotely similar about us. Where I stand tall, he's just over five feet. His small stature and trim frame in opposition to mine. I grew up a thin girl. Adulthood gifted me a new body with curves and a butt. Still waiting on the boobs, though.

The guys all *ooh* in unison, rocking into their seats with laughter.

It was interesting joining homicide. I'd already been under Sal's wing for years at that point. The fear that one of my kills would end up on one of our desks made me the first to jump at any murder case. Funny, no fear of death, only being trapped behind metal bars for life. Cops that end up in prison don't last long.

I may be immortal, but rebirth is a painful ordeal. As I took a new breath, the bones and tissues broke apart. The individual molecules separating only to resettle anew. For weeks, my body remembered its reformation. Learning its improved form.

"Anything good, fellas?" I chuckle as I collapse into my seat, Gomez already handing me a piping cup of coffee. I should chug some water, but the near-black stimulant steaming in this mug wins.

"Nothing new yet, but those weird cases always seem to find their way to you," Garrett Booth, one of the younger homicide detectives, scoffs.

He's the type I would take home. Almost considered it once when he asked me on a date. He's tall, dark, and handsome. The complexion of an Egyptian god, chiseled bone structure, and deep-set hazel eyes. As fun as it would be, I keep business separate from *my* pleasure. The last thing I need is for him to know any of my secrets.

My shoulders tighten just the slightest at his joke. He's referring to the tall stack of unsolved murders. A large chunk of them are my own handy work. The hours spent trying to link them together, a waste. The search for a signature, pointless.

I am the serial killer they're looking for. My kills were all carried out with opportunity weapons. The less messy, the better. Getting blood out of clothing fucking sucks.

"Weirdo magnet, I am."

A forced laugh escapes as I power on my computer, knowing there will be a mountain of emails waiting for me. There always are. Random tips or the Medical Examiner's office with results or Forensics sending along information for the many cases Gomez and I still have open. For every case we haven't solved yet — most being mine — we've closed three others. Our solve rate trumps the rest of the department. The sole reason our captain lets us get away with the shit we pull most of the time.

The morning passes in a whirlwind before Captain Barlow comes in, dropping a folder on my desk. "Luxembohrg. Gomez. Hot one for you." He's the only one that uses my full last name. Everyone else opting for the shorter version, Luxe.

"What's the rundown?" I ask, my brows knitting together, reading through the thin file.

A small sigh of relief leaves me as I realize it's not one of mine. No, this one was a murder in a residential home in Lincoln Park, where the houses cost millions and the soccer moms take mid-morning walks with their strollers.

"Middle-aged couple found stabbed repeatedly in their home. Neighbor found them. When she called through the front door, no one answered. Let herself in and found them both in the living room. No signs of forced entry. Only thing we know for sure is homicide."

Grabbing my coat from the back of my chair, I'm nearly running to the elevators. Gomez understands I love the thrill of solving a crime. There's no time to waste. The longer it takes for us to get to the crime scene, the more it will be altered. CSI will take what they need, swabbing and photos and bagging, preserving what they can. Likely EMS dirtied up the place, too.

It takes a solid thirty minutes for us to reach the crime scene; the area taped off in the bright yellow streamers blocking the public from getting closer. An officer meets us at the edge, spewing off everything Captain Barlow already told us. I wave him off. His lack of pertinent information not helpful. These rookie cops can be the worst. I should be able to sympathize with them. I was one once, but I don't. They just get in my way and piss me off. I learned how to be helpful early in my career. It would be best if they learned to do the same.

Turning into the living room, blood spatter coats nearly every surface. The *drip, drip, drip,* of it from the coffee table onto the cream carpet, louder than it should be amongst the voices and shuffle of bodies.

Deep breath. Close your eyes. Listen. Feel it.

My mantra before I take in every crime scene. When my eyes open again, everyone fades away. The noise and live bodies. The nuances of what happened here coming into view with vivid clarity. As if the scene rewinds and replays itself for me. The husband was incapacitated first. He's on his back now, but I would bet my life there's a stab wound along his spine. The first wound for him. Once down, he'd rolled over, attempting to protect himself, only to take the knife to the gut, shoulder, throat, thigh, and cheek. The face had been just before his heart stopped. Only a trickle of blood slipped free.

His wife heard the commotion running in after him. The angling of her body tells the story. She found the culprit still crouched over her husband. It was then she tried to run. The assailant slammed her head into the molding, the small chip of paint stark in contrast to the gory laceration and her skin tone. She'd fought back. Her arms and hands mutilated with defensive marks.

My heart breaks for these people. Faces similar enough to mine to pass for my parents. The man's eye shape. The woman's nose and hair color. It's the sliver of her irises that makes me stumble, colliding with a CSI behind me. The narrow strip of navy blue, so much like my own.

No, Ari. You're just seeing what you want to see. It's not her.

Five

A chill trickles down my spine — one I can't shake — as the images of that couple flash through my mind. Their faces seared into my brain. This isn't the first time I've looked into the faces of strangers and wondered if they were my parents. If I had looked into the eyes of the people who brought me into this world and left me alone.

"What's the deal, Luxe?" Gomez asks as he idles in the traffic along Lake Shore Drive, exactly where we'll be sitting for at least another hour.

"That woman's eyes..." My voice trails off, locked on the luxury condos just outside my window.

With a heavy sigh, Gomez drops a hand to my thigh. The most paternal touch a man could give. Gomez is a touchy-feely person, but there's never been anything uncomfortable about it. He has four young kids and a wife he's been married to since he was eighteen. He's always been a comfort though, someone I would call a friend if I let anyone actually be one. "It's not them, Ari."

Using my first name pivots the conversation from business to personal. One of companions that share secrets and provide reassurances even if they're making promises they can't keep.

"But... I've never seen eyes my color on another person."

Gomez laughs. The sort you give your child when they tell you something outrageous, but you just might go along with it. "Ari, there are millions of people who might have navy blue eyes and you've never met them."

I know he's right, but I still push, unable to shake the feeling creeping up inside me.

"Yeah, but are any of them a black woman with my nose?"

He says nothing more, as we inch through traffic, blaring horns filling the pregnant silence between us.

I don't stick around once we get back to the office. Heading home to become one with my balcony and bourbon once more. I can't shake their faces. Can't stop thinking about them or staring at the photos from the crime scene in the file as I sip my drink. The burn is so good. Its heat provides me with the focus it should strip away.

I'm blanketed in the dark of my balcony when I come to. The folder still clutched in my hand and my glass empty. It's not unusual for me to fall asleep outdoors when on a fresh case. The sounds of the city and the brush of the wind against my cheeks help me think. Clarity I can only find here or at the lakefront.

Buzzing deep beneath the pillow pulls me from my thoughts, my fingers probing for where my phone is wedged under me. The caller ID tells me everything I need to know as I press the green button.

"My house. Ten p.m." *Click*. Sal's voice already faded into the night. I'm only called to his residence when he has a mark considered a VIP.

I still have two hours. His condo building being only three blocks away from my own is enough of a comfort for me to sink back into the cushions. Coincidence? I don't know, but it sure is convenient when he calls his dog to heel.

Flipping open the file folder again, I skip past the crime scene photos and go straight to the one depicting the happy family. The woman, Syriah James, flanked by her son, Tucker James, and husband, Lanham James. They were a beautiful family, bright smiles flashing. The file revealing they were in their sixties, the features of their pleasant faces telling a different story. One of youth like my own.

They could be my parents.

They're old enough.

Shaking my head as if it will clear the thoughts, I flip through the pages again.

The son, Tucker, lives in the city too. An area where quaint homes line the streets. He's only three years younger than me. The light waves on his scalp and curve of his brow, reminding me of my own.

Slamming the folder closed, hands running through my wind-blown hair, I exhale a loud breath. I've spent so long looking for my family. It's no wonder I see it in every face. Willing similar features and skin tones and smiles to be a match for my DNA. I'm not alone then.

Gomez is right. I'm seeing what I want to see.

I need to focus on the facts. Solve this case just like all the others.

A hot shower, large pizza, and two cups of coffee later, I'm riding the private elevator up to Sal's penthouse. He lives in a place most only dream of. It's not that I couldn't afford it. But what would I do with a two-story penthouse? It's just me. No one to share it with. He at least has a wife, unconditionally devoted to him, and three grown children of his own.

"Drink?" he asks as I step into the foyer.

I don't miss him eyeing my attire. Skinny jeans may be my go-to, but Salvatore has a dress code for entering his home. My trendy suit, with the off-center zipper and wide-leg slacks topped with black Louboutins, seems to appease him.

"I'm good." I raise a hand to wave him off. "Who is it?"

There's no point beating around the bush. Sal prefers my simplicity. My forward nature to get straight to the point. No time to waste. With a smirk — a glass of red in one hand — he grabs his iPad with the other, lowering it into my palms like priceless crystal.

The face of my next target greets me. The man with eyes like emeralds is gorgeous in contrast to the overweight grimy drug lord that was my last assignment. A jaw so chiseled it might be carved from stone. Thick sandy brown waves wild atop his head. His only soft feature, the copper freckles speckled across his proud nose. His stature tells me he's strong, not only physically but in his mind, too. The scowl he wears indicates just how much bullshit he's willing to put up with. None.

"Any information?"

"Already sent."

With a nod, I hand him back the iPad. Long bony fingers curl around the edge of the device before dropping it onto the sofa next to him.

"Time?"

Sal always has a deadline. There are no open ends to his requests. He wants what he wants when he wants it. A guarantee I can make him, while he carries out his dark plans for world domination.

"Three weeks."

There's no hiding the widening of my eyes. That's one of the shortest time frames he's given, but it's no never mind. I like a challenge.

Six

Nearly two weeks have passed. The dueling halves of my life warring with one another. My search for another murderer that isn't me versus the next hit on my list for Salvatore. Dark circles pool in the puffiness under my eyes. My hair — normally tamed into submission — becomes frizzy, tucked into a tiny ponytail. One that barely contains the short stray hairs that like to fly free at my temples. The worst is my temper. Flaring at even the most minuscule of things, all while enduring the looks of pity from Gomez every time he catches me staring at the photos of the James family.

It's a feeling I can't shake. A force taking hold inside me. Telling me I'm connected to these people somehow. Maybe they aren't my parents, but there are unexplainable ties that bind us. There's a familiarity in their features and the way they hold their posture in the family photo. More than once, as I prep myself for the minimal hours of restless sleep, I stand in the mirror analyzing the way I hold my shoulders or the curve of my nose or jaw. It's not just the hue of the blue, but even every sliver of silver matches the now-dead woman.

Tonight is the first Gomez and I haven't pounded the pavement until well past nine, giving me time to trail my next target, Adrian Alexander. The type of name that accompanies models and movie stars, not accountants. Those that crunch numbers for fun — and a living — come with names like Bob and Joe. Just my luck, Adrian's gorgeous features match his sexy name. Even memorizing his squeaky-clean background makes my libido hum. A sensation I can't say I've felt before hunting any of my targets.

Much like me, he leaves the office late at night, checking his surroundings discreetly before he leisurely makes his trek home. His office is in the heart of downtown, a tall onyx building of glass along Wacker Drive. The streets are busy enough this time of night, making it easier for me to blend and weave through the throng of bodies as I follow him.

I'd yet to track him home, as he often visits other places before finally tucking in for the night, but tonight it seems luck is on my side. He heads for the L Train, his satchel slapping against his thigh, as he looks left to right once more — this time more obvious as if he wants people to notice. *Interesting.*

For a boring accountant that seems to live a clean life, he checks his surroundings an awful lot. Some dark secret hidden beneath his polished image. Good enough reason for me to be even more careful as I trail him. Hunt him, like the prey he is. No matter the outcome, I have my trusty dusty detective badge I can always rely on. Though, without finding a single indiscretion on the man, I can't imagine what sort of lie I would tell to go with it.

He boards the train; me following just close enough that he's long since seated himself at the far end, his back to where I now stand by the doors. He may be my target, but I'm in no way disillusioned that Salvatore doesn't have his own enemies. One gunning for his hitwoman before she can come for them. You hear the whispers loud and clear through the dark underworld I often ingratiate myself into. As far as I know, no one definitively knows my identity, but I can't put trust in assumptions.

The chill of the breeze hits me as we deboard the train. Still Adrian doesn't seem to notice me as he makes his way from the station and toward the streets littered with homes. Each different than the last. As if each owner hired a different architect from their neighbor just to be unique.

We weave through the quieter streets of Lakeview. That familiar churn of Lake Michigan waves in the distance soothing me. As counterproductive as it is for a Firebird to love the water, I do. The sounds and smells and spray always being what I crave most in my human and bird forms.

I'm lost in my own thoughts, my focus frayed — an unusual occurrence for me — when I nearly expose myself to Adrian as he unlocks the front door to an unassuming brick home on the corner of West Wellington Avenue. Darkness stands firm behind the sheer-curtained windows as endless minutes stretch by. Using the shadows of a large oak on the corner, I wait. Expecting lights to surface on the main level first, I'm surprised when a front room on the upper level becomes illuminated. The shadow of the man should be dancing across the curtains, giving me a peep show. There are no shadows.

I've learned to be a patient woman, keeping my shoulder pressed against the flaking tree trunk. For the second time tonight my mind wanders, eyes latched onto the lone lit room in the house. It's enough that I don't hear the nearly silent footsteps behind me, or have time to react as a large hand snakes across my nose and mouth or the arm that wraps around my waist.

Heat roars through my body, my Phoenix itching to break free and rescue me. Tonight it won't be necessary. I can defend myself, except his grip is unyielding as he drags me through the gate at the back of the house and inside. I expect him to attack or subdue me. But he releases me the moment we're through the door, locking the several latches and a bolt. Panting, my hands stay braced against the granite countertops, my back still to the man that just dragged me inside.

"Care to tell me why you've been following me, Detective Luxembohrg?"

My eyes shut tight, my lips pressed together so as not to curse audibly — my cover now blown. In all my years doing what I do, not once has anyone ever figured it out until it was too late. A gun to their temple or knife at their throat. Not once was I ever made before I chose to reveal myself. Their own personal grim reaper already on their doorstep.

Slowly turning, hands still gripping the counter, I stare down the Adonis before me. He looks like a fucking Greek god in a cheap suit and I know what he makes annually, so there's no need for him to wear something so ill-fitting.

"How long?"

His eyes squint. He knows what I'm asking. How long he's known I've been following. The urge to ask what gave me away is like an itch that can't be scratched. My refusal to show any weakness the only thing keeping me from clawing at my forearms. If I play my cards right, I can likely end this asshole tonight. Salvatore has always rewarded early delivery with a couple extra hundred thousand and a longer break between kills. I could use one about now.

"Since day one. I could sense you."

I have no idea what he means. *Sense me?* Like he's some sort of trained dog that could sniff me out. It's becoming clearer there's more than meets the eye with this one. Something dangerous hidden there beneath the surface. A threat to Salvatore. *Not my problem*. I just need to get my job done. Clean kill. No sign of me being here. Simple.

"That's great. Look, Mr. Alexander." The use of his last name the only respect I'll show him. "If you know who I am and that I've been following you, then you know why I'm here. I would suggest you make it easy for me."

In an instant he's in my space, that brick-hard body pressing mine into the countertop, long strong fingers wrapped around my slender neck. His nose less than an inch from my own as trembling breaths escape into the space between us. There's no fear. Only an attempt to restrain the temper he's clearly fighting to hold on to. His fingers tighten, ever so slightly, just a shred of my air supply inhibited.

"Ms. Luxembohrg, I would suggest you get out of my house before you regret coming here in the first place."

His hand releases in an instant, the force throwing my head back. He shares no further words or even a look as he casually strides from the kitchen, up the stairs, and out of sight. The quiver in my hands is enough to stop me from following him.

Exiting the way he carried me in, I stay in the shadows. I'm near the gate when a vibrant blue flash of color catches my eye. A single feather fluttering in the grass near the fence. It's not the feather of just any common bird. I know it. It's the same as mine. A single. Phoenix. Feather.

Seven

"I need more time."

I swallow loudly, waiting for Salvatore's answer. I've never asked for an extension, but it feels necessary now, as I twirl the blue feather between my fingers. It took me three days to buck up the courage to call him. Three days to decide if trying to pursue someone who might be like me or know where I can find others like me was worth pissing Sal off enough that he may no longer see me fit to be amongst the living. Little does he know he can't kill me. I would just rather not be hunted for life.

"Reason?"

I'd practiced this in my mind. Over and over. What I would say. How I would justify the need for extra weeks — not days. "There's a reason you want him dead. I don't need to know it. But in the weeks I've been hunting him, there's clearly more we don't know. Let me get you additional intel. Then I'll sweeten the deal and dispose of anyone else in his group you want gone, too. Free of charge."

Silence greets me on the other end of the line. No background noise. Not even Salvatore's breathing as he ponders what I've asked of him. I have every intention of dispatching Adrian once I've got the answers I need. The chance of finding even just one more creature like me is too good to pass up, though. It's like the cure to my loneliness has been presented to me on a silver platter and I would be a fool to say "No, thank you."

"How long?" he finally asks, his words punctuated by a dramatic sigh.

"Another three weeks."

"Fine." The line goes dead, but at least I've bought myself more time.

Today was one from hell. Gomez and I called it quits early, so that gives me plenty of time to wander back to Adrian's house. It's just past dusk as I slip in through the back door, my memory recalling what types of locks held it shut. It's odd that he would have so many, but again I need to remind myself he has more to hide than he lets on.

Once I've snuck into his home, breath held deep in my lungs, listening for any sign of other inhabitants, I wait. Minutes tick by, remaining statue-still until I'm satisfied I'm here alone. Despite the house looking narrow from the front, it's quite large on the inside, sporting seven bedrooms, four bathrooms, and even a basement. The house is decorated in a sophisticated fashion, all white and shades of gray. It's quite dull actually but fits that of an accountant. Despite the sculptures and paintings on the walls adding to the elegance, there's no personality here. Nothing that tells me more than I already know.

Taking up my favorite position while waiting for one of my victims to come home, I settle into an armchair in the living area, darkness creeping over me. Hours must pass before the telltale click of the front door unlocking pulls me from my haze of thought. I expect only Adrian to enter, but he's not alone, as Tucker James and another female the size of a large child walk in behind him.

There's no conversation as they enter the house, casually shoving the door shut. "You could have turned on the light," Adrian sighs in my direction before the fluorescent glow of energy-efficient light nearly blinds me.

"I wanted to surprise you," I snicker, hands resting on the arms of the chair.

Eyes of cerulean blue stare at me. Tucker's eyes. His lips press into a thin line. If I thought my eyes were unusual for a black person, he definitely has me beat. They're brighter than the photo lets on. His features more masculine and strong with time since the picture was taken.

"And you are?" the female asks me.

Not bothering to even pay her any mind, my focus turns to Adrian. His face devoid of any sign of what he might actually be thinking.

"My new stalker, apparently," he sighs before dropping his bag to the floor.

The girl's eyes go wide as she takes in Adrian's words. Her small stature and blonde waist-length hair making her appear unimposing.

"We need to talk," I say, pulling the conversation back in the direction I need it to go. "They need to leave."

Neither Tucker nor the girl move. Adrian makes no attempt to dismiss them, simply settling into the middle of the sectional couch in front of me. His elbows rest on his knees, fingers steepled beneath his chin as he continues to stare me down. Discomfort flares under his scrutinous stare, not only because he seems so unfazed finding me here, but because all I want to do is mount the man right here and now. I clearly need to go find another rando in a bar tonight.

"How did you find me? I've been looking for you for years."

It's my turn for my eyes to gouge themselves from my head. Tucker's words dancing through the space around us. *Find me. Why?* How is he connected to all of this with Salvatore? Not to mention his parents were just murdered with no sign of who the perpetrator was.

"Like I said, I need to talk to Adrian. Leave."

"If you recall, this is my house. They stay. You speak." Glaring at him once more, he continues. "You don't like it..." He shrugs, popping out his lower lip. *Fuck. Him.* "You can go, but this is your one chance to ask whatever stupid questions you have. I won't let you back in again."

Let me back in. This motherfucker. How dare he talk to me like I am some simple child. I broke in. *Me.* I shouldn't be proud of that being a homicide detective and all, but I am. It took time to learn the art of being discreet and getting into the sacred spaces of peoples' lives. The places where I shouldn't have been.

Pulling the feather from the inner pocket of my leather jacket, I twirl it between my fingers. Much like I've done for the past three days. Watching the slight iridescence glimmer in the light like flecks of tiny glitter. All three of their faces stay stoic as they watch my fascination with the single feather. Only when I pull out a second, one of fire engine red and copper, does Tucker suck in a gasp of air.

"So, since we're all staying. Care to explain to me who this feather belongs to and where I can find them?"

Silence. Soul-crushing, deafening silence.

Eight

Silence surrounds us. My rapid breathing and the steady pace of the three of them staring back at me the only sound to break it. My impatience grows as I wait, only Tucker showing any outward signs that he's on the cusp of breaking. Of letting the floodgates open to either put me in my place or spill all his secrets. I'm wagering on the latter by the uneasy shift of his eyes and the brief twitch of his long fingers against his thin thighs.

It's easy to see what type of frame Tucker has. Strong, lean, almost stretched as he towers over the girl. His clothes fit him perfectly as if designed for someone with his build. Yet his shoulders remain as broad as his chest. The angle of his jaw would make him look like a vicious villain if his anxiety wasn't peeking through.

"Well?" I question, waiting for someone to give me some sort of response to my inquiry.

Tucker takes a breath, ready to speak, stopped only by Adrian holding his hand out. A signal for him to keep his mouth shut.

Tucker obliges, making no effort to fight against Adrian's request.

"Ari, we owe you no explanation."

"But —" Tucker tries again, taking a single step in Adrian's direction. Another hand halts him mid-step, his enormous foot suspended mid-air.

"What are you?" Adrian asks me.

His question unsettles me for a moment. The unexpected, thrown back at me. A question I couldn't have prepared for. My arrogance blinding me once more when it comes to Adrian Alexander.

Narrowing my eyes at Adrian, I toss the question back. "What are you?"

A wide grin spreads across his face as he leans back into the cushions, his legs spreading wide in his charcoal slacks. "You're holding my feather, so you already know." Long arms spread across the back of the couch, my mouth hanging open at the obvious answer he just gave me.

"You're like me?" The words whisper past my lips before I can stop them.

All these years, I've been so alone. Thinking I was the only one. That there were no others like me, only to learn that a mere twenty minutes away, there was another of my kind.

"Did you know?" I breathe.

"Not at first. Not for sure until I found you lurking outside my house." The nonchalance in his response makes my blood boil. Those flames licking beneath the surface.

"And you weren't going to say anything?"

"No."

The single word makes me want to throttle him. Tear at his perfect hair and wrap my fingers around his throat as he did to me only days ago. Thank goodness I heal quickly and it's cold out, otherwise, I wouldn't have been able to hide the bruises he left behind.

"Well. That's it then." Planting my hands on the arms of the chair, I move to stand. Ready to get away from this asshole as fast as I can. He may be like me, but I'd rather be lonely than have to spend extra time with him.

Yet I still owe Salvatore his death and he's the only one who may be able to give me answers. The double-edged sword of this situation unjustly conflicting in my mind. Locking eyes with Tucker and the girl, I suddenly remember their presence and I know at that moment they are like me, too.

"If you're a Phoenix..." my eyes locked on Tucker. "How were your parents murdered?" He doesn't answer right away. His eyes filling with unshed tears.

On a deep breath, he gives me yet another dose of honesty I wasn't ready for when I came here tonight. "*Our* father wasn't a Phoenix. Mythical being, yes, but not like us. *Our* mother still lives."

Our. That word implies more than one. Surely not Adrian or this girl. They look nothing like Tucker, but maybe for non-humans genetics don't work the same. The phenotype, inconsequential — yes, I studied genetics too, another attempt at trying to make sense of what I am.

"Who is *ours*?" I ask, already sure I know the answer.

Tucker takes several sure steps toward me, extending his hands as if he wants me to take them. I don't.

"Ari, you're my sister. I've been looking for you for years. I'm your younger brother."

The world drops out from beneath me. My knees buckle as I tumble back into the chair I'd just been in.

"Great, now that we've had our family reunion. We have business to tend to. You might be one of us, *Ari*..." My name spews off Adrian's lips like a curse. "But anyone who breaks into my home with the intent to murder me for Salvatore Danarius isn't welcome in my home, so kindly get the fuck out."

Shock at tonight's revelations and the hope blossoming in my chest make it so I barely register Adrian's words. Only when he stomps over, grabs me by the biceps and marches me toward the front door — Tucker on his heels pleading — do I slither out of my stupor, tearing from his grasp.

"I'll enjoy killing you when the time comes, especially if you ever forcefully put your hands on me again. I don't care who you think you are." Turning so I'm chest-to-chest with Adrian's giant body, I press in close. "If you ever manhandle me again, I will be sure it's the last thing you do."

I'm met with nothing but a smirk as the front door opens and I'm shoved out, nearly colliding face-first with the pavement under my feet.

Fuck. Him. And his poor attitude too!

An unfamiliar feeling tugs at my insides as I stand at the curb. It's been years since I felt it. Years since I was unsure of my purpose or what to do. How to move forward in the way that would benefit me best. What would put me in a position of protecting myself while still trying to get answers to who my family is; why I am what I am?

Standing in the cold with only the soft glow of the streetlamp above, I'm lost. Time passes quickly. Slowly. I'm unsure. Only the numbing of my fingers tucked tightly into my pockets brings me out of my meaningless thoughts. There's no haste in my steps as I make my way to the train station, retreating the same way I came.

I've gained only a few feet of distance before I hear slapping footsteps behind me. Then a hand on my shoulder. In any other circumstance, I would have broken someone's hand, wrist, or arm for even thinking of touching me unwarranted. There's no fight left in me tonight, as the owner turns me to face him. *Tucker.*

"Ari, I'm so sorry. I tried to talk sense into Adrian." I have no response, as he stares at me, studying the features that so closely resemble his. My brother. I have a brother. And a mother still living. "Let me take you home."

A nod is my only response as Tucker leads me to a sleek black sedan. Don't ask me the make and model. I wouldn't know. Cars aren't my thing. Why do I need a fancy fast set of wheels when my wings can carry me so much further, so much faster? When they offer me freedom, no other mode of transportation can.

Nine

Tucker's quick to speak as we slip into his car, the purr of the engine softer, quieter than that of my 4Runner or my Mustang. "Our parents are something like royalty in the paranormal domain. They hold a lot of power. Power men like Salvatore Danarius want to control."

At the mention of Sal's name, my head whips around, an audible gasp escaping me before I can stop it.

"What does Sal have to do with all of this?"

Tucker's brow quirks in confusion, his true focus never leaving the densely packed city streets of Chicago. I should ask him if he needs directions, but I don't. The opportunity to hear the secrets this stranger seems willing to spill, overshadows the need to return to my lonely apartment unharmed. An internal pull inside me tells me I'm safe with this man that claims to be my brother. That same part of me knows it's the undeniable truth. No proof needed.

Settled deeper into my seat, my gut begins to uncoil. Thirsty for the information Tucker has for me. Secrets that I feel entitled to as his sister. As another phoenix.

"You're serious?" Disbelief wrapped tightly around his words.

"No, I'm asking because it's fun."

A chuckle comes from Tucker, his long fingers curling around the steering wheel before loosening again. Braced at ten and two like a new driver. It's astonishing how young he appears, almost like a teenager, but with the carriage of a full-grown man. I know he's twenty-nine, three years younger than me. A time difference that barely qualifies as a gap, yet the chasm of time seems vast. Impossible to bridge having spent our lives apart.

The weight of my current life status threatens to crush me. My target is a phoenix, too. Finding my brother. Learning my mother is my case — just like I thought—and not actually dead. Let's not forget there's a whole supernatural world I never knew existed, but should have because what I am is real. *Twilight* and *Underworld* — my favorite movie franchises of all time—immediately comes to mind, hordes of werewolves and vampires fighting one another. I know better. The term paranormal crafted to define those that resemble humankind, but come equipped with other magical gifts, expands far beyond the Twihards.

"You're so much like Mom. Equipped with a viper's venom and sharp bite."

My brow scrunches at his analogy. Comparing us to a snake. My mind takes the comment as a show of disrespect. The need to slap him stupid, making me tuck my hands beneath my thighs. He knows her and I need to remember that. I don't. I know the Luxembohrgs who raised me. Then let me fly free — figuratively and literally — when I left for college at eighteen and never came back.

"Salvatore?" My teeth grind painfully as I attempt to piece together what my boss has to do with any of this.

"He's a warlock. There is a balance that should be maintained, but some are greedy. Some want more and they do what they can to take just that. Salvatore is one of them. Each species has a ruling family, for lack of better terms, in each country. Our father was also a warlock, a creature easily killed, but not our mother, despite Salvatore's efforts."

I sit quietly, listening. Thinking back to the endless murders I've committed for him. How many were "different" like me? How many were just humans whose lives I stole to further whatever agenda that greedy asshole has been running for who knows how long? How many lives have I destroyed for him?

Tucker continues, "With our parents gone, as well as many other high-ranking paranormals in the world, Salvatore can ease himself into power using force."

He doesn't have to add *easily*. The implication is clear in tone and word choice. Something other than indifference settles in my gut for the first time.

"How, if he's only a warlock? Can't he only be the ruling body for them, from what you just said?"

"Not if everyone fears death by his cronies, which I understand you are."

The muscles of Tucker's jaw tick repeatedly. His words like a knife to the throat. A blunt exclamation of what I do... what I've done, not sitting well with him. Why would it? I've been executing for some sadistic pig. I knew Salvatore had big ambitions. Why else would he have me kill the ones I have? Sadly, I always knew I wasn't his only, just the one reserved for higher priority targets.

"Yes, I've been on Salvatore's... payroll for seven years now." A hard swallow follows, fear forcing hesitation at asking the next bit of information I want to know. "Do you know the ones I've killed?"

He shakes his head, those fingers tightening once more before pulling to a stop at the curb. He'd brought me straight home. How he knew where I lived, I don't know. As if he can read my mind — maybe he can — he answers, "Adrian knew your address. Just like you've been following him, he was doing some digging into you, as well. He suspected you were... different, but couldn't tell what, uh, kind until he got close to you."

It's suddenly clear why he dragged me into his house that night. A chance to analyze me the way I have been with him. An opportunity to get close. To learn what I am. I'd read that creatures like us can sense the same in another, or just "other."

"And no, I don't know who you've killed." Sadness settles into Tucker's eyes and his hands drop to his lap. "But Adrian will need to know. You'll meet him tomorrow at seven p.m. to review each one." I nod, reaching for the door handle. There's no protest left in me.

"Tucker, one more question." The swivel of his head back in my direction, quick. One of my booted feet already planted outside the car. "If Adrian is a phoenix and we can't die..." My words fizzle out before I can continue. "How did Salvatore think I was going to kill him?"

"Did he ever give you a special weapon? Gun? Knife? Told you to always carry it with you on kills and use it if someone is difficult?"

My heart seizes in my chest. The words from my brother's lips nearly matched the ones Sal delivered to me so many years ago. The custom Glock and bullets cradled into my eager hands. He said he usually hands out knives, but I seemed like a gun girl. He'd placed the weapon in my hands and given me those exact instructions Tucker just recited. Now, the dense plastic just seems to burn as it digs into the soft skin of my lower back. The location I often keep it.

With a nod, I exit the car, hearing Tucker's last words before I shut the door. "He'll be here tomorrow at seven." Then he's gone, pulling away from the curb and disappearing around a corner. Feet rooted to the sidewalk beneath them, the wind whipping my dark waves against my cheeks, my eyes remain trained on the city before me. A city I thought I knew.

I'm getting so much more than I bargained for.

Ten

Gomez has been regurgitating information at me all morning. His words in one ear and out the other. With a deep breath, I do my best to refocus. Today's trip to the morgue will hopefully provide us with some answers. The Chief Medical Examiner requesting we trek out to the office specifically to review her findings.

Assistant ME, Dr. Sharon Maurin, had already signed off on the release of Syriah's body to the family to be cremated. There was nothing of note other than various stab wounds and a head laceration. Exactly what we saw at the scene. Cause of death exsanguination. Manner, homicide. Simple. Clean. Only I know there was no cremation. At least not one she didn't rise from when no one was looking.

It's not Syriah we're here for. It's Lanham. Chief Medical Examiner, Natalia Ridolochan, called us in this morning, the quiver in her voice enough to make us move. "Dr. R, what do you have for us?"

Both Gomez and I shake her hand as we follow her down the white hallway, cast in shadows and scented with bleach and formaldehyde. Oddly enough, it's one of my favorite smells. The number one reason I loved so many of my science classes in college. I was the only double major in Biology and Ancient History and Mythology. An odd combination, as reported by my advisor. Her making it crystal clear she believed the history portion to be a waste of time when I was going to be a doctor. She didn't understand. No one did and I couldn't tell them. Being a phoenix has always been my secret. Alone. Until last night.

"Well, it's odd. With the number of stab wounds Mr. James incurred, he should have bled out. He didn't. He may have appeared dead at the scene, but his heart was still beating, so slowly, I presume, no one would have ever picked it up. No machine could have picked it up. It's almost as if he's suspended in time. Like his body is frozen in a state of pre-death. I can't explain it. Nor have I ever seen something like it. But see for yourself."

Shoving open the double metal doors of the examination suite, Lanham's body lies on the silver metal table in the center of the room. His chest and abdomen flayed open like a fish. Majority of his organs are still in place, but it's his heart that Dr. Ridolochan points to.

"Watch. Closely. Don't blink or you'll miss it."

Gomez looks like he's ready to vomit. He's never been great with dead bodies or the smells of the morgue. For me, it feels like home. Somewhere I always should have been. Yet, I believe I'm meant to be a detective, too. It seems we are meant to be many things in this life. Or maybe that's just me.

The silence blankets us, barely blinking, eyes drying by the second as we watch. As we wait. Then Lanham's heart beats. Just a single tiny flex. My dad's heart beats. Tears burn behind my eyes. Tucker was wrong. Our dad is alive, but I have no idea how.

Gomez drives us back to the station. I don't stay, stating I have a few things I need to look into. I really just want to be alone. The need to release the shuddering breath that escapes me the moment the lock to my apartment clicks shut, near crippling. Back pressed to the door, I sink to the floor. How the fuck has my life completely shifted on its axis overnight? Everything has changed and I don't know how to process any of it.

I'm slow to rise from the floor. Dropping my phone and gun on the kitchen island as I shuffle down the hall to my bedroom. A quick shower later and I'm wrapped in the softest sweats I own. My feet warm in my socks as I nuzzle into the couch. I let my thoughts wander again, figuring I'll just lie here until Adrian arrives.

I know I'm not alone. The only truth I can latch onto with confidence. I have a family. There are others like me. *I am not alone.* My final thought, as my eyes close, hands tucked under my cheek, cuddling into my microfiber couch.

Darkness surrounds me when I wake again, the insistent knocking on my door making me bolt upright. Wiping the string of drool from the corner of my mouth, I stumble through the dark toward the noise.

Adrian stands there, a bag of Chinese in one hand, dressed casually in a hoodie and dark-wash jeans. *Fuck my life.* How is this man even sexier in his casual clothes?

"Are you going to let me in?"

Nearly tumbling backward, my socks slipping on the hardwood, I move out of the way, the door creaking as I pull it wider.

"Did you not pay your electric bill, or are you a wannabe vampire?"

The warmth that had been pooling between my legs at the sight of him quickly chills to ice. He's such an ass. Like he intentionally just wants to irk my nerves because he can. Flicking on the light, I guide him to the kitchen, pulling dishes from the cabinets and silverware from the drawers.

"Definitely wannabe vampire," I scoff, dropping everything in front of him.

I don't wait for his response as I head back to the couch, sprawling out while he plates his food. My forearm drapes across my eyes, the light an unwelcome intrusion after the four-hour nap I took.

The clash of a plate against my coffee table draws my eyes back open. "Try not to break my shit —" My words stop short when I see he made me a plate too. A mix of beef and broccoli, shrimp fried rice, egg rolls, and chicken lo mein smothering every surface of the oversized dishes.

"Didn't know what you like, but I'm starving and it's going to be a long night."

The fog clearing I remember the real reason for Adrian gracing me with his presence. I leave for the second bedroom I use as an office. He doesn't pause slurping down noodles and chugging his glass of water, as I drop the stack of kills on the table between us. The weight enough, my table does a little wobble as they hit. The silverware jingling to drown out his chewing.

"Thanks."

My only response as I scarf down my food as if I've never eaten before. Truth be told, I forgot to eat today. Even on the days when I remember, I devour calories like a linebacker. Men are always either disgusted or shocked that I don't order a salad to keep my fit cop bod and instead prefer greasy and fried. I'm not thin by any means, but I keep. So far the poor food choices haven't caught up with me, so I just keep doing what I do.

This is the first time I've been self-conscious about a man watching me chew with my mouth open or inhaling my entire plate in five minutes. Adrian's gaze bores into me, mouth open and fork poised as he was just about to take a bite.

"What? Salvatore doesn't pay you enough to eat?"

The raging boil of my blood surges through my veins again as I drop my fork and plate back to the table. "What the fuck is your problem?" Perched on the edge of the couch, I'm ready to throttle Adrian once again. He raises my temper and gets me hot and bothered in more ways than one. It's insufferable and infuriating.

"Other than the fact that you're still planning to kill me for Salvatore, none at all, Princess."

"Well, I'm not thrilled to be in your company, either. So, let's get this over with so we can be done with one another."

Adrian looks like he is going to respond, before he glugs the rest of his water, heading to the kitchen to refill it. He returns only moments later, the condensation already beading against the clear glass, before grabbing both our plates and filling those again, too.

He releases a sigh as he returns with two equally stacked plates. Gently placing mine back on the table with a grunt. "Eat first. Then we work. I'm not dealing with your hangry attitude if I don't have to."

"Dick," I whisper under my breath as I clear my second full plate of greasy deliciousness.

"I heard you."

"Good."

There are no more words shared between us as we both finish our meals. Only stolen glances of me glaring at him under my thick lashes. No response from him, though. Not once do I catch him looking anywhere but at the plate of food cradled in his hands. Where I eat like a caveman, he's all controlled poise, wiping his mouth more times than I'd care to count.

Once we've finished, he pulls the first sheet off the stack. I'd prepared for this after Tucker dropped me off last night. Printing the summary sheet for every kill, one by one. Looking into the eyes of everyone I've murdered the past seven years tightens the knot at the base of my belly. Kills for a mission I didn't even bother to understand. I did as I was told. A loyal soldier. The only way to feel alive while my bird stayed trapped inside.

He asks about each one. Details and whereabouts. I hadn't even noticed the laptop case he walked in with until he pulled his Mac free, diving into databases. Getting through the first twenty took us well past midnight, attempting to piece together Salvatore's plan. Tying together what each — paranormal and human alike — could potentially give Sal with their deaths.

"I'll be back tomorrow night to go through the next bunch." Adrian shoves his laptop into his bag.

"Can't wait." Sarcasm thick in my tone.

"Lock up that petulant attitude. I'm not going to put up with it."

Fuck. Him. Fuck. Him.

No one. No man talks to me like that. "Let me be clear about something, Adrian. I'm not killing you... yet—" My eyes trail up and down his body, attempting to look like a menace, but more than likely only achieving lovesick teenager. "I am helping you, but you're not going to be an asshole to me. I don't care how you talk to other people, who the fuck you think you are, but I'm not the one."

His face nears mine, our noses nearly touching. "Let me be clear, Ari. You answer to me. Want to know who sits below your parents? I do. So get in line and stop pushing my motherfucking buttons."

He's already got the door open. His foot across the threshold. The temptation to let the door slam into him is strong, but I don't give in to the impulse.

"Text me what you want for dinner." His version of goodbye as he saunters down the hall, leaving me to watch him go.

Eleven

A week of Adrian showing up at my place promptly at seven, a bag of takeout in hand, becomes my norm. I forget that I have a deadline. He's still my target. His constant attitude making me want to murder him most days.

Baby Got Back blares through the car. My phone coming to life in my pocket. Gomez eyes me but doesn't ask as I answer it.

"You're late." His growl sounds through the speaker.

Gomez's brows nearly touch his hairline as he hears Adrian's voice. I keep my personal life pretty private. Keeping my sex life away from the guys' eager ears. My life is simple. Sex. Murder. Solve cases. There will be questions when a man's voice comes through the Bluetooth oozing bitterness.

My night routine, once he leaves, has become finding randos in the bar to fuck the aggression out of my system. No one raises my blood pressure the way Adrian does. Lucky me, the guy from a few weeks ago was there Friday night. David — I think that's his name — so I haven't had to find someone new for days. The downside is that the guy wants to take me on an actual date. *No, thank you.*

"I'll be home soon. Let yourself in."

Gomez is still staring at me when I hang up. "Who was that?"

"My brother." An immediate response. A stupid one, because I've never talked about my adopted family. Not in detail. I was their only child, that much I'm sure I've said before.

"Brother?" Gomez throws me a knowing look. Lips pursing and eyebrow raising again. "Look, I don't need to know, but he needs to watch how he speaks to you."

One of the many reasons I love Gomez. Always defending my honor. The unofficial brother I've gained since being partnered with him.

"I've got it. Promise."

I throw him a wink before peeling out of the car and waving him off. Most days I don't drive to the office. I would rather walk. Feel that Chicago breeze on my face. It gives me time to think. Time to forget the horrible things I see and the equally unforgiving things I do. I find perspective and healing and clarity. Not tonight, though. Tonight, all I can think about is sitting side by side with Adrian for the eighth day in a row. His pine scent filling my nostrils while I try to focus on doing what I can to help.

Our dynamic remains tumultuous. He's a bigger dick than ever. Our tempers flare at the tiniest details. I've seen Tucker a few times for lunch this week, his plea to stop testing Adrian falling on deaf ears. It's not my fault. He's the one with the snotty remarks and underhanded comments. No hesitation in revealing everything he disapproves of when it comes to me. His repeated jabs that the Phoenixes are lucky Tucker exists because I would never be fit to lead them. That one hurts the most.

Not because I want to lead. I barely understand this "other" world. Only because all I've ever wanted is to belong. To have a family and be wanted and loved. Sure, the Luxembohrgs did that. They've always given me nothing but love even as I've stayed away all these years, but it's not quite the same. They aren't like me.

Adrian's stretched out on the couch when I enter, a chill making me shiver as I close the door behind me. "Steak's in the oven."

"Thanks," I call, stripping off my coat as I make my way to the bedroom.

I've been in these clothes all day. All I want are fuzzy socks, sweatpants, and a baggy sweatshirt.

It never occurs to me to close the bedroom door. Adrian has no reason to come this way. Yet, the sound of his voice behind me has butterflies coming to life in the depths of my belly. My heart erratically pumping in my chest.

"Hurry up," he grunts.

Spinning around to face him, I completely ignore the fact that I'm in a lacy bralette and panties to match. Electric blue ones at that. That same knowing smirk pulls at the corner of his mouth, his thick arm resting against the doorframe as his eyes scan my body. The heat of a flush creeps over my skin. Heat that belongs to my libido when it should be from my anger.

This ass barged into my private space without *my* permission.

"Get the hell out of my bedroom, you creep."

"Or what?"

A taunt. A dare. Well, two can play that game. I'm so sick and tired of Adrian Alexander. Marching straight to him, chin angled up to make up for the height difference, my eyes narrow to slits.

The distance provided by being on the other side of the room solidified my plan. Ready to tell him off for coming into my private space. I was ready to put him in his place, but as I stand in front of him, our chests nearly brushing, my nipples pebbling beneath the lace fabric, his jaw ticking in time to my pulse, I don't have words. His head tilts to the side, lowering closer to mine. Nearly nose-to-nose. Our daily face-off.

"Or. What?" he drawls, his warm breath spreading across my lips.

An audible gulp is my only response as he knots his fingers in my hair, lips crashing into mine. I'm still for a moment, unsure of what's happening, as he breathes me in. Only when his lips move do mine follow, my hands snaking around his waist and pressing flat against his back, pulling him flush against me. The bulge behind the fly of his jeans tells me just how much he's attracted to me. Is this like when you're in elementary school and boys tormenting you equates to a crush?

His lips sculpt around mine, drawing a moan out of me. One hand drifts under my barely covered butt cheek as he hoists me into the air, my legs wrapping around his waist. Even as my back slams into the doorframe, our mouths stay glued together. Our tongues warring as we do with our words. His torso flexes as my hips roll against the planes of muscle.

My skin is on fire. So hot, I need to open my eyes to be sure I haven't actually caught flame. I've ruined several cute tops that way.

His lips leave mine, tongue tracing along my jaw before he whispers my name in my ear. The heat already pooling between my legs becoming molten lava.

My name being called by a familiar male voice as my front door slams shut pulls me back to earth.

The spell is broken. Hatred fills my eyes once more as I glare at Adrian, pounding at his chest to release me.

"Ari, where are you?" Tuck calls from down the hall.

"Just — Just a minute," I stammer, shoving Adrian out of my way, as I slip into the clothes I pulled out. Nearly running from the room, I leave him standing there, finger-combing my hair as I hustle down the hallway. For once, I am thanking the gods above for lips so full collagen injections could have created them. Hopeful that Tuck won't notice they're swollen from my momentary lapse in judgment.

As I skid into the living room, I find Tucker and Talia waiting. Just like the night I first met her, her pin-straight blonde hair hangs loose, shimmering in the light. His girlfriend of three years. Now equipped with that knowledge, it was so clear. How they angled their bodies just enough to protect one another. He told me she's a phoenix too, but where our birds resemble fire, and Adrian's the hues of the ocean, hers has the greens of a garden. Each bloodline comes with gifts. The feather color eludes to what elements they originate from. She even brought me a feather so I could see for myself. A show of faith.

Just as I pull up the sleeves of my sweatshirt, I feel Adrian behind me. Tuck's face shifting to disbelief.

"Come on, man, that's my sister."

Kill me now.

Twelve

Talia's eyes dart between mine and Adrian's, then back to mine, skipping to Tuck's as she takes a loud slurp of her green smoothie. It's rare to see the girl without one in her hand. Rather, it's amusing how much she values only ingesting healthy meals and clean fruits and veggies — certified organic — when sickness can't touch her. Still, she never wavers. Sweets rarely cross her radar and she eats nothing fried.

"So..." That single word drawn out so long I wonder if she'll have to catch her breath after she lets go of the note. A mischievous gleam sparkles behind her eyes, self-restraint wrapping her slips around the straw before she says anything more.

"Nothing happened," I snarl, marching toward the kitchen. The container with my dinner slaps onto the counter, the aroma of the medium-well meat making me salivate. I'm careful to keep my back to the group. I can't bear to see the look on Tucker's face. Whether it be anger or excitement or disappointment. I've always wanted a family. He's my brother and I only want him to love me. Real-life to match the fantasy in my head.

Talia's opinion matters much less, but I know she's important in our community. Her actual role is unclear to me, other than knowing she is a genius when it comes to hacking and all things IT. She is the sole brain behind the database Adrian and I have been sifting through that harbors the information on every known paranormal in existence.

Hushed words are shared between Tuck and Adrian as Talia joins me in the kitchen. She says nothing as I shovel tender filet mignon and red-skinned mashed potatoes into my mouth. Her sipping her smoothie forcing the grind of my molars. "You know he's our leader until your mother can come out of hiding, right?"

Glancing her way, mid-chew, I pause. I do know. Deep down, but hearing her put into words — Adrian's real importance — makes my pulse race. The time he has spent sequestered in my apartment instead of stepping up to lead. It almost makes me forgive what an ass he is, but stubbornness wins. I refuse to accept his newfound responsibilities as an excuse for his behavior.

"I'm aware."

I wince at the bite in my tone. I've got no qualms with Talia. She's been insanely helpful introducing me to a world I thought I alone lived in. The small O of her mouth revealed her shock at what I did and didn't know. There wasn't much that surprised me. Only the nuances of the creatures that roam in the shadows. Hidden from the humans that fail to realize there's truth to the movies. The myths and legends that shouldn't exist. But for me since age ten — maybe even before that — I already knew did.

"Then you should know, it's best that you steer clear. He needs to focus. We have too many enemies against us right now. To be honest, none of us have really decided if you are one of them or not."

With a quick quirk of her doll-like mouth, she hops from the counter, sauntering back into the living room. Her soft lilt drifting from the room beyond. "Enough boys. We have work to do."

Taking advantage of my last few minutes alone, I remain rooted in place. The food I'd been consuming only moments before turning unappetizing. A flavor akin to dirt, not a red wine reduction. Pushing the lid closed, I join the crew in the living room.

Tucker's seated in one armchair, his glare pointed solely at Adrian. Talia sits on the arm of his chair, rubbing soothing circles into his back. It's clear they aren't working as Tuck shuffles through the remaining stack of my targets.

"You messed up the order." I race over, pulling the sheets from his hands. Hoping none of them tear, even though it would only take me moments to reprint them. The protectiveness of my indiscretions drives my outburst.

"Sorry," he mumbles, slouching into the pillows.

There are only two options for seating. The floor or the couch near Adrian. Neither is appealing.

"Learn to wipe your face," he growls, as I do my best to reorder the papers.

"Screw. *You!*"

Talia and Tuck groan in unison, her unsure words whispered into the quiet tension. "Are you sure you guys aren't sleeping together...?"

"No!" we both bark in unison.

Clearing her throat, and pulling her own laptop from a bag, she mumbles, "Maybe you should."

It's my turn to grimace in her direction. That... What happened between Adrian and me tonight was a hormone-driven mistake. My libido is just a greedy little whore and latched onto the first breathing male in sight. These stress-filled days might be the death of me. His excuse, I was the only option present. Sure, I can admit I am wildly attracted to his handsome looks, but his attitude is worse than dog shit. Let's not forget Talia just warned me away.

"Do you know who this is?"

Tuck holds up a photo of my last kill. Mario Silarno. I can still picture what a filthy mess he'd been that night. One of the few drug lords I've never had the pleasure of investigating as a detective. One not afraid to get his hands dirty as he beat his carrier to within an inch of his life in the alley before coming home that night. I'd watched from the shadows. His fists. The slick metal bar that had been lying near them repeatedly thumped against the bone and tissue of a guy no older than twenty.

Watching that scene play out, I'd been more than happy to end Silarno's life. To erase him from this planet. I see something different now. Those electric amber eyes stare back at me from the page. I know without a shadow of a doubt he was like me. Like us. A phoenix.

"How did you kill him?" Adrian asks his body angling toward me, knee brushing against my thigh, sending a tingle down my spine.

My eyes close, a deep inhale filling my burning lungs. I should have known. The gun was different. Its weight heavier than it should have been. The catch with the pull of the trigger. A millisecond delay that isn't there with a normal gun. I was so eager to end the poor fool's life; I ignored all the details. The specific scent that I've always associated with my Firebird, filled the space of that room. The one true giveaway.

"His own gun. One similar to mine," I mutter. The words draining the life from me. "He was the last hit ordered by Salvatore before you."

"How many others have been phoenixes?" Talia asks.

"Twenty-four out of the seventy-two we've sorted through so far," Adrian answers, his fingers pushing against tired eyes.

"And others?"

"Ten werewolves, two vampires, fourteen witches and warlocks, three other animal shifters, one siren, and the rest humans."

A curse escapes Tuck as Talia pulls him into a hug. Her fingers swirling through the short waves atop his head.

"What do we do?" Exhaustion infused into my words.

"You will do your part and help walk through each one of these you've murdered, then I don't give a fuck what you do. Just stay out of my way."

The shove at Adrian's chest barely moves him, my temper flaring once more. "You can get out of my house."

"Apartment," he corrects, moving on to the next victim.

"Get. Out." I point at the door, my torso arched over him. He remains unaffected by another of my outbursts. His attention stays trained on his computer screen, completely ignoring my raging disposition. I'm over the disrespect.

"Let's call it a night," Talia coos, pulling Tuck to his feet.

"We've barely gotten anything done. We need to figure this out sooner rather than later," Tuck retorts.

"Now," Talia gives an unnatural grin. Tuck finally follows her to the door with a groan.

"I'll see you tomorrow. Lunch?"

"Please." I smile.

I truly have loved Tuck's company. Getting to know him and our parents. We're not the siblings who hug yet. Our relationship barely beyond that of strangers, so an awkward wave is all we share.

Adrian is still typing away on his laptop when I turn back to him. "I told *you* to get out."

"Doesn't seem like you want me to leave at all," he drones, eyes still narrowed on whatever holds his focus.

"Well, I do." The fight to maintain my anger versus frustration is a losing battle.

"Your panties say otherwise," he grins.

Thirteen

Another week slips by. Tuck and Talia playing chaperon for Adrian and me. That's exactly what it is, no matter which way they try to cut it. The excuses of "we just want to help" and "we *all* need to figure this out together" are weak. Their best attempt at keeping us from physically clawing at one another's throats.

Tuck is always here to serve as the guaranteed buffer, picking me up most nights. I tried to bring up what he thinks he witnessed, but I'm cut off at every turn. His warning is the same as Talia's *stay away from Adrian*. Although our bickering has lessened with the passing days, I don't like Adrian anymore than I did the day Sal sent me to kill him.

The weight of the clock ticking down hovers over me. That dark cloud ever-present. Trapping me in a cage I can't find my way out of. Salvatore wants his head, no exceptions. No excuses. I'm not sure how I'll get out of it. How I'll pull the coup of all time. I may not be a fan of Adrian, but I won't kill him. I refuse to murder any other paranormals. Let Salvatore come for me. His life is much easier to take.

"Where's your head at?" Tuck asks me, turning onto a residential street in the suburbs we've never been on.

"Nowhere. Everywhere."

"Penny for those thoughts."

I throw him a small smile, my skull pressed into the cushy headrest. I'd been so lost trying to find a solution to my Sal problem, I hadn't noticed that we weren't going to Adrian's house. A small prize when I announced I wouldn't kill him under any circumstances two nights ago. He'd stared into my eyes, testing me. Searching for the truth. He found it. His only show of kindness, allowing be back in to his home.

"Where are we going?"

Tuck lets out a chuckle. His smile wide, displaying large white teeth, whereas mine was small, reserved, nearly nonexistent. "There's someone you should meet."

He pulls up outside a large home in the cul-de-sac of the long residential street. Where the other homes are large, and many newly remodeled, this one is massive. Its appearance more similar to that of a castle than anything modern.

Leading me to the front door, he doesn't knock before putting in a code, followed by his thumbprint. The clicks and brushes of metals seem loud in the early evening, the mechanism within whirring with life. A final thunk sounds, the door shifting open a breath before Tuck pushes it wide.

The space is brimming with immaculate pieces. The decor akin to something out of the Palace of Versailles. It is impossible to not fall into the attraction of this place. Fingers tracing over every surface. Like walking into a private museum. For a history geek like myself, it's nearly orgasmic. My mind already tracing the origin of the side tables, paintings, and vases welcoming me.

"Like it?" Tuck bends to whisper in my ear.

I need no words as a huge smile spreads across my face, a nod shaking my waves wild.

A woman rounds the corner. Her navy blue eyes well with tears the moment she sees me. Syriah James. My mother. *My. Mother.* Without thinking, we run for each other, like in the movies where the family gets reunited after what seems like a lifetime apart. Her powerful arms wrap around me as she pulls me close. Her scent one that seems so familiar, like the waves of the ocean. But I couldn't remember her. I was barely four months old when the Luxembohrgs found and adopted me.

Holding me at arm's length, she finally pulls away. The tears left unshed now streaming down her face. A gorgeous face. One so similar to mine.

"I'd hoped I would find you someday," she sniffles, hugging me close once more. I hold her back, intent on never letting go. Long moments pass before we finally release each other. A single tear slipping free, wiped away by her finger. She leads me by the hand, down a hallway with paintings of beautiful nature settings dancing with life. "You must be hungry. Adrian tells me you never stop eating."

Rolling my eyes at her back, I keep my lips pressed tight. Focused on making a decent first impression, I choke down my hateful words reserved solely for Adrian Alexander. Just my luck. He's seated just ahead — at the kitchen island — his phone in hand, back to me as I enter.

"Hello, Adrian," I coo at his side.

"Sweet boy, Ari has finally arrived." My mom streaks a hand across Adrian's cheek. Sweet is not a word I would ever use to describe this asshole. For the second time, I keep my mouth shut. She clearly has a soft spot for him. "Thank you so much for looking after my little girl."

The groan from Tuck pulls all of our attention, but my mother's smile never breaks. "Boys, go set the table. Ari and I will plate everything and bring it into the dining room."

They do as she says, while I assist my mom around the kitchen. She quickly learns that my domestic skills are lacking, but she never stops talking to me. Asking me questions about my life, keeping it strictly to work. Not once does she mention her case. Or what I've been working on with Adrian. She asks me if I have a boyfriend and what he's like. Her cheeks glowing with excitement. That's the only time a pang of hurt squeezes my chest, as sadness springs to her eyes. "Oh sweetheart, you shouldn't be so alone."

If only she knew how alone I've been all this time. How it nearly consumed me and ruined me as the years flew by. How I carelessly sleep with too many men to cure it and drink too much bourbon to drown it out. The way I've searched my entire life for them, for anyone like me. How the kiss with Adrian a week ago was the first time I felt anything remotely good. Like I fit with someone.

Dinner passes slowly, the laughter never dying down. My mother and the other elder phoenixes, seated with us, do their best to make Tuck and Adrian blush the entire time. My brother is the youngest at the table, something I wasn't expecting. I was sure Talia was younger than him based on looks alone but came to find she's almost ten years older. I was convinced Adrian only had a few years on me, too. Although he refused to divulge his actual age, it's made clear he's seen several centuries. *Mind blown.*

It's been decided that we'll all stay at the house tonight. A safe haven for any in need. There are several of them across the state sanctioned by my parents and the ruling families. It's where my mother has been hiding out all this time. Only those on a short list knew.

"Here's your room." She ushers me into an ostentatious room of midnight splashed with gold.

"Um... Mrs. James —"

Her eyes narrow, hands wrapped around my biceps in a vise grip. "I may not have been there to raise you. It should never have taken us so long to find one another. I won't force you to call me mom, but you can if you'd like." There's hope in her eyes. An eagerness to hear the simple word slip past my lips.

I nod. Daring myself to test the word. "Mom..." Pause. "Mom," I breathe, less shake to my voice. "Mom." A third try. "Can we talk in the morning? Just you and me?"

I feel like a little girl asking for permission to play with my toys. A vulnerability on display I haven't allowed for years.

"Of course. We'll go walk along the beach." She kisses my forehead before hugging me once more and disappearing down the hall.

Skulking into the room, I kick my boots off on the way to the bed, removing my blouse and unbuttoning my slacks as I go. There are silk pajamas laid out for me and toiletries waiting in the bathroom. Clad in nothing but my undergarments, I head for the en suite bathroom.

A pale gray high wing-backed chair sits in the corner. The lights are not lit, so I initially missed the hulking form lounging in it.

The flick of the switch reveals my visitor. My heart in my throat as Adrian stares back at me. His posture so regal all he needs is a crown of jewels.

"Are you kidding me? You nearly gave me another heart attack. What is it with you and being in people's bedrooms without permission?"

I'm racing for the bed, attempting to slip the nightshirt over my head and hide my body from him. One he's already seen plenty of.

"Just yours."

An audible sigh escapes me, my head falling back in exhaustion and frustration. "Adrian, I am in no mood to fight with you tonight. Can you please go?"

"Who said anything about a fight?" A wicked grin pulls at those lips. Lips I wouldn't mind kissing again. "I just want to... talk."

Immediate dampness seeps into my panties and I know I'm in trouble. If I don't put distance between us, I will not be able to keep my hands to myself, so grabbing the bottoms from the bed, I run. Down the hall. Down the stairs. As far away from Adrian Alexander as I can get.

Fourteen

The cold bites at my exposed skin. Frost already collecting on the individual strands of grass tickling the bare soles of my feet. The silk pajama set does little to stave off the chill, forcing me to call on the flames that live beneath the surface. The warmth slowly replacing the severe frigid air.

Deep breaths fill my lungs. It's not that I'm out of shape, but unless I am chasing criminals, I don't run. If you see me running, run too — far away. It's the one activity that can control my temper. Saved for when I've traveled to a land so far past rage, even a good fuck can't wind me down. Times my bird threatens to free itself so I can escape everything holding me down.

"We're going to need to work on your speed."

My eyes shut, blocking out the sexiest voice I've ever heard.

"I'll add it to the list of reasons you think I suck," I murmur, the sarcasm drenching every word like viscous honey.

I'm usually so sure of myself. Confident in who I am and my abilities. So sure of what I do and don't want. Until Adrian is near me. Then I question everything. Not because of my sexual attraction to him. That fucker being the first to foresee me coming, threw me so far off balance I can't right myself again.

Those feelings of inadequacy bubble to the surface. Their origins reach all the way back to growing up an orphan — thankfully, adopted by lovely people — but believing my family didn't want me.

It's been a treacherous fight, overcoming those feelings. Stomping them to a pulp so deep inside me, they would never surface again. Adrian destroyed it all in one night. His long fingers wrapped around my neck. Demolishing any notions that I'm stealthy in following my targets. In his presence, I am the prey. Him the deadly predator.

"Can you just disappear?"

His low chuckle fills the space beside me. Still clad in the same casual wear he wore at dinner, hands tucked into his jeans pockets, shoulders hunched against his powerful jaw, he takes a step closer. Close enough our shoulders nearly brush, as his scent fills my nostrils. As much as he infuriates me, he also makes me feel alive. So much less alone. I hate it.

"You know, I just came to tell you I think I know what Salvatore is up to."

With a huff, I turn to him, arms crossed against my chest. Partially a show of defiance and partially to stave off the winds whipping at my back. "And knocking on my door after I was dressed was such a stretch?"

"It's more fun to see you frazzled," he snickers. That gorgeous face dipping close to mine. Our noses nearly touch, just before he pulls back again, turning away from me. Eyes focused on the trees beyond, the waves of Lake Michigan rolling in the distance.

"Well, out with it. It's freezing out here."

"You're the one who ran out here nearly naked. Not my fault you lack the common sense of a child."

My blood is boiling. The flames that I usually keep at bay threaten to break free across my flesh. *Not the time.* Regardless of the fact that my current attire does little to keep me warm, I would prefer not to walk back into the house in nothing more than my birthday suit. *Deep breaths.* The fresh air filters in through my nostrils and out past my now chapping lips.

Without prompting, Adrian removes his thick sweater. It's impossible not to watch out of the corner of my eye, attempting to keep my cool. Keep my distance.

Why the hell is he undressing out here?

"Lift your arms, Ari," he orders. His tone that of how you would command a child to obey. The desire to pout is overwhelming, but I refuse to give him that kind of satisfaction. I refuse to let him hold that kind of power over me.

As if aiming to touch as much of me as he can, he lowers the sweater over my head, freeing my hair from the hole before sliding his hands down my arms and sides as he lets the thick warmth surround me. Wanting to throw my arms around him for the bit of kindness, I instead clench my fists at my sides. This asshole deserves nothing from me. A nod of thanks is all I'm willing to give as the words start flowing from him.

"There's a balance that has to be kept amongst the paranormals. Each region has a 'ruling' body, per se." His fingers form air quotes. "Then each country has its own council of regional leaders. Every three decades a new member from those councils is a representative of the world council. It's a delicate political puzzle. Your parents are the regional leaders for both the warlocks, witches, and phoenix species. Many thought it was a power play on their part when they first announced their engagement. Two species coming together with the bloodlines and power they possess unheard of."

"Is that what it was?" The words fly from my mouth before I can catch them. All I've wanted is to know my family my entire life. Now, without prompting, Adrian is offering a piece of them willingly to me.

"No. Not at all. "

A shiver wracks my body, teeth chattering. Even my internal flames do nothing to combat the fierce winds. Taking my hand in his, Adrian leads us back into the house. Directly upstairs and into the warmth of my bedroom. He's silent as he moves us to the small sofa against the far wall, pulling a blanket from a closet I hadn't even seen and draping it over me.

"So, like I was saying. It wasn't a power play. Has Tucker told you anything about how our species find their life partners?"

I shake my head. Our conversations were charged with funny stories about him growing up and boundless curiosity about me. Sprinkled with the years of him searching for his sister. Assuring himself that I was still alive. That I was still here.

"For our kind, it's the Pairing." With a quirk of the corner of his mouth, he gazes at me. "Original, I know. Anyhow, it's very common among creatures such as us and vampires, warlocks, etc. Rarely does it happen between different species, but that's exactly what happened to your parents. Once that bond is formed, it's unbreakable."

"How do you know you've Paired with someone?"

"Your magic calls to them. It's like an invisible rope tethering you together. It's impossible to stay away. To see anyone else. It'll always be there even if you choose someone else. There's only one way to lock it into place."

Idly, I wonder what that one thing is. What could possibly further anchor you to someone that your soul already belongs to? If that's what it really is. All the crazy mating stuff I'd read in books is real. I'm suddenly curious if Adrian has gone through this. If there's someone that holds the very core of who he is? Whether or not he chose her.

"Have you gone through... it?" I'm unable to find the right words. Too nervous to ask if there's someone in the background. Someone who had been waiting for him when he kissed me that night.

He pauses. His eyes unsure for the first time since I met him. His Adam's apple bobbing with his swallow. "I have a Pair, but have not locked in the bond."

He says nothing more for long moments. Sitting beside me in silence before continuing his story.

"Your parents were one of Salvatore's targets. I assume you know you're not his only hitwoman?" A nod of acknowledgment. "Looking at the list of targets you've had, the paranormals he's specifically targeting were higher-ranking individuals with unique gifts, but your parents are the only leaders so far. However, then looking at his human picks, it became clearer."

"Well, don't leave me in suspense." I'm not sure I want to hear what he has to say. Yet, I need to. The urge to understand what I am going against by not killing Adrian as planned.

"Simply put, a takeover of the paranormals. With the right ones on your side, it's possible to access the powers or magic within other paranormals, especially as a warlock. If he can acquire the magic someone like your parents have coupled with the other enterprises, such as the drug and gun trade he has been taking over, there will be no choice but to bow to him."

"What's the point, though? This sounds like a bad X-Men movie."

"Wish I knew." His teeth audibly grinding.

There it is. The root of Adrian's frustration. The core of mine. We can't prepare for what we don't know. What we don't understand.

Fifteen

Shimmering morning light drifts through the parted curtains rousing me from sleep. I'm still snuggled under the plush comforter, wrapped in Adrian's sweater. The soft material still smells like him. My resolve to hate him faded a bit with his honesty last night. An openness he's always been reluctant to share with me. He's still an absolute ass, but if he's willing to give me the information I need, I can deal with that. Make this whole "partnership" work for me.

A soft knock at the door sounds before my mother enters, a small smile playing on her lips. Her eyes drift to the sweater my body drowns in, a knowing smirk follows.

"I'm glad you're up." Her steps are sure but feather-light as she saunters to the bed, balancing herself on the edge. "Why don't you get dressed? There's so much we should talk about."

With a nod, I scoot out past her, aiming straight for the en suite bathroom. I don't bother showering, simply tying my loose waves back from my face, before conducting my ridiculous skin-care routine — the products I normally use all lined up on the countertop as if I was expected to stay all along. Aiming for casual, I slip into skinny jeans, knee-high boots, and a wine-colored knit sweater.

My mother is right where I left her. Eyes focused on nothing in particular. I studied her face last night. My face, someday. Even though the woman before me barely looks five years older, I know from Tuck she's nearly eighty. A difficult concept for me to wrap my mind around. How slow we age. Our time on this earth monumentally longer than our human cousins.

Without a word, she guides me through the house. Past the same back doors, I ran through the night before. Our steps taking us across the wide field of grass and directly into the trees. I don't question where she leads us, but I'm careful to look for markers. Bread crumbs to guide me back should something go wrong. A hidden attack or this woman who has shown me nothing but kindness turning into my enemy.

She finally stops in a wide clearing encircled by trees that seem taller than average. A spot that can only be manmade, the perimeter perfectly curved. The dense woods shelter its location from easily being seen. The treetops so high, the sky seems further away than usual. Taking my hands in hers, my mother looks into my eyes.

"I never thought I'd see you again. See the woman you've become. Tucker knew, though. He always believed he'd find you."

Tears well in my eyes, matching hers. The same navy blue eyes with silver flecks I've looked into my entire life. An endless search to find the one with a pair to match.

"I knew when I saw your eyes at the crime scene... I knew who you were then. Even when my partner said I was imagining it."

She gives a soft smile, her hands rubbing over my own. "We do have a unique coloring, courtesy of your grandfather." My heart beats a little faster. Hope building in my chest that I'll meet him soon. As if knowing the direction of my thoughts, she answers. "He passed some years back, my sweet girl."

I do my best to hide the sadness. The opportunity to meet my entire family torn from me before I had the chance.

"Uh, Mo —" The word stalls in my throat. *Mom*. All I've ever wanted was to know my mother, to call her mom. "Mrs. James," I try again. "What happened when I was a baby?"

With a sigh, she settles onto the chilled ground, legs folded beneath her. "It was a tumultuous time between the werewolves and our kind. They attacked our safe house in the middle of the night. Shifters of any type have always had a hard time seeing eye to eye. We all made it out alive, but the one who was responsible for getting you to the next safe house never showed. We never saw him again. There were no signs of what became of you. We searched for years before..."

Her words trail off. *Before giving up.* She doesn't have to tell me how that sentence ended. Before determining, I was nothing more than a lost cause. Dead or taken. No longer worth coming after.

I am not an emotional person. The tears fall just the same. All those feelings of not being enough to hunt for — not being wanted — come rushing back. Full force. The tidal wave drowning me along with the chill in the air.

"Oh, sweetheart. We never gave up on you. Not even for a second. There were other issues to deal with. Assassinations against our kind and other paranormals, dwindling our numbers, our families, *our* people. As council members, your father and I had to maintain those duties, too. So when we found you —" Her fingers brush under my chin, lifting my gaze to hers. Those matching eyes stare back at me. "You had a world worth living in to come back to."

I hug her then, arms draped around her slender neck. Her small hands rubbing my back through the sweater. We stay latched to one another for more time than I would have imagined.

"Now." Her hands pat my thighs. "We have some catching up to do. Today and tomorrow you'll learn from me. Then Oliver Borneo, our Training Officer, will spend time with you as much as your work schedule allows. We all grew up among the phoenixes, but you didn't. I want you to know how to protect yourself." Her fingers graze my cheek. My shoulders tensed for the icy touch. Instead, I'm greeted with eternal warmth.

Moments later, my mother's shift begins. A marvelous sight I've never actually seen. Only read in books or seen animated depictions of. Her fingers elongate transitioning into the feathers of her Phoenix. The same shades of radiant flames as mine. Where I thought my wingspan broad, hers is nearly double the length. It only takes minutes for her bird to stand before me, those piercing blue eyes brighter now. Her expectant stare the nudge for me to do the same.

I can't remember the last time I'd let my phoenix soar. The last time, I let it free. It takes longer than it used to for me to channel it, to call it forward. Feeling the heat simmer and my pulse slow, it makes its way to the surface. The anatomy of my human skeleton stretching to become expansive wings, my lips turning into my beak and my small child-like teeth becoming sharp daggers inside my enlarged mouth.

With a nod, my mother ascends toward the cloudless skies. That's when it hits me. What this place is. There is a reason the treetops sit so close to the heavens. Why the clearing spreads so wide. Not wasting another second, I charge into the air after her.

For once, happiness floods my chest.

This is me.

This is home.

Sixteen

Turns out Phoenix training is so much harder than regular workouts. There's a soreness that lingers. My bones and tissues unfamiliar with the constant changing I'd done over the past week. My mother and Oliver — one of the funniest men I've ever met — assure me in time I'll get used to it. That my body will fully understand what I am.

As it is, I did myself a huge disservice treating my bird the way I have. Keeping her cooped up and letting her fly only when my human side deemed it appropriate. To become the real me, I need to accept that my Phoenix knows what's best for the both of us. This human shell of a body a disguise, but the Phoenix is the true heart of who I am. A heart of fire and feathers. My truth. It's the very essence of everything I am.

My free time is filled with Oliver's grueling regimen. A welcome reprieve from Adrian's sour attitude. A small mercy. Seeing him at all is a reminder that I'm past my deadline, delivering his death to Sal's doorstep. I've done my best to play this as carefully as I can. It's still a secret to most that my parents aren't really dead. Well, my mother, at least. None of us really understand what my father did to himself to keep him frozen between the land of the living and the dead.

As if on cue, my phone rings. "Luxembohrg," I answer, knowing full well it's Salvatore on the other end of the line. My heart rate races, but I call to my bird to slow it. To take control. Just as Oliver taught me.

"You're late."

"I've got more cases than usual. Complicated ones. I need more time."

Silence greets me, but I hear the grinding of his teeth. See the scowl on his face while he makes me sweat out his response.

"I like you, Ari. This time I will let it slide. My place tomorrow night. I would like a full update on everything you've found. *All* of it."

The line clicks dead. Sweat dripping down my scalp, snaking through the hair at the nape of my neck. The room is suddenly stifling. The air too thick to draw into my lungs.

I do the only thing that might help. I text Tuck.

Me: *Salvatore knows.*

His response is immediate. The ellipses dance at the bottom of the screen. His messages appearing in rapid succession.

Tucker: *How do you know?*

> Tucker: *What did he say?*

> Tucker: *Adrian will pick you up after work.*

> Tucker: *Meet at the safe house.*

> Tucker: *Why aren't you answering?*

> Tucker: *Ari*

> Tucker: *Ari?*

> Tucker: *ARI! Answer. Me!*

> Me: *Well if you gave me a chance to respond I would.*

> Tucker: *I'll see you tonight.*

His panicked responses leave me chuckling to myself.

There should be no room for laughter. No place for amusement, but despite Tuck being younger than me, he's become a fierce protector. Just two days ago, he caught Oliver and me, huddled together in laughter, his rangy arm stretched across my shoulders. His brotherly speech only made our laughter roar louder. Oliver is almost a hundred years old. Yet Tuck and his twenty-nine years thought he could put him in his place.

He'd been spot on, though. Oliver and I bonded quickly. His cool and charming demeanor won me over. A drastic difference between the desperate men who fuck anything with a hole from the bar and Adrian's broody ass. Our conversation comes easily, and he's done amazing teaching me how to master my skills. Even honing some of the magic I didn't even know I had, thanks to my dad's bloodline.

That same night, he'd ask me to grab a bite with him. I'm always starving, so the natural answer was yes. It was nice to have a friend that I could joke with. An ally who knew the real me. Who knows what I am and looks at me with pride. I'm not sure I should be making nice with the Training Officer, but it's been lonely, with only Tuck and Talia welcoming me into the fray. Many of the others look at me with distrust. The hatred and skepticism swirling in the scrutinous glares.

That night, walking out of the training facility, an old warehouse on Division Street, Adrian caught sight of us. Anger flared his nostrils and etched his normally beautiful features into something deadly. A lesser woman would have feared what was clearly his way of showing jealousy. I just pulled Oliver closer, arm tucked around his waist, my wave dismissive of Adrian's attitude.

The day passes in a blur. Gomez is out due to his youngest having some sort of stomach virus. I love kids but when they get sick, *gag*. I hadn't lied to Salvatore when I said our caseload had grown. More and more murders fill the files lining our desks, some similar to the ones I'd done myself, others similar to the James'. There's no reduction in the basic ones either. Gang, drug, and domestic violence crimes continue to multiply. Either way, my desk is littered with folders and cases that all need my attention.

It's after eight when my phone buzzes, pulling me away from the deep dive I'd been lost in. The endless lines of digital communications never-ending.

> Adrian: *You have 2 minutes to get out here before I drag you out.*

Fuck him. Just to spite him, I stay put. Reading through lines and lines of messages between the suspect and his victim, a middle-aged woman clearly starved for attention. There's nothing but pity in my heart for her. The world tells us as women we are useless if we're over the age of thirty, not married, and without kids. Deemed undesirable if not in the workforce, maintaining the home, and raising demon children. Such bullshit.

My heart jumps into my throat as Adrian's voice sounds behind me. "I said let's go. I have better things to do than be your chauffeur."

Turning in my chair, a smirk pulls at my lips. "Then go. I do have my *own* cars. I can get myself to the house."

"Get up, Ari. I'm not in the mood for your games. Or would you prefer to slaughter me here?"

Something like hurt blossoms in my chest. I may not be nice to him, but how could he think I am still willing to kill him? I made it very clear I would do no such thing. That I would protect him and make sure I kept him safe the best I could. Yet this fucker throws it back in my face every chance he gets. I told Tucker because I thought he could help. That he could make this better.

"Fuck you, Adrian. Get out of my precinct."

He charges me before I can react, his body bowed over mine as my rolling chair presses back into the desk. My body follows suit to create as much space as I can between our faces. Adrian's warm breath coats my skin. My heart is racing in anticipation. A part of me hopes those firm lips brush mine. That he touches me at all. The muscles between my thighs pulsing with want.

His nose skims my neck, lips brushing my earlobe as he gives me orders. "I don't answer to *you*. I don't care who your parents are or if you're fucking an officer. Get out of this damn chair and let's go."

How dare he presume I'm sleeping with Oliver. Not that I wouldn't, but still. My hand draws back. The crack of my palm landing with enough force to snap his head to the side. Pink blossoming.

"Talk to me like that again Alexander, and I will have your balls next."

Pushing him aside, I grab my purse and stalk outside, right past his car. Straight to my apartment.

I'll drive my damn self.

Seventeen

Entering the safe house is like walking into the circus. Bodies everywhere. Many faces I don't recognize, but many that I do.

"Everyone downstairs," a voice calls. The masses stomp down to the basement, across the expansive room, and then down another flight of stairs hidden behind the wall.

I had no idea this much basement existed. Logically, I knew a house like this likely included more space than I'd seen, but this is out of this world. My only reason for coming down here previously has been use of the gym, it's location clear on the other side of this mega-mansion.

Grave faces line the front of the room, Syriah James at the forefront. The leaders of the vampires, werewolves, warlocks and witches, sirens, and animal shifters a feathers width behind her. The varying faces are only a small group of representatives. So many others exist in the world, gathered in the countries where their lore originated from. Oliver throws a small smile my way, earning a scowl from Adrian, as he catches me grinning back.

"Salvatore Danarius has been after us for a long time. We will take greater precautions moving forward. Luckily, with the holidays lingering close, we will be able to remove the young and those unable to defend themselves discreetly. Our human counterparts won't notice. In the meantime, we've come into some knowledge of Salvatore's current kill list. We already knew Adrian Alexander is one due to him being Ari, my daughter's target, but we've gathered other names now."

My mother's voice arches across the room. Commanding her audience, pulling them all in with curiosity. Their gazes shifting my way for mere seconds at the mention of my name.

A man with dark eyes and darker hair steps out of a group, gray peppering his beard and thick locks. "And how did you come upon this list?" His accent is pronounced. The skepticism clear in his voice. Distrust a thick fog filling the room. We hold our breath, the illusion of oxygen being sucked from the room keeping us still.

"Bronson, bring him in." A warlock specialized in binding spells comes into view, with another man walking straight-legged in front of him. There are no cuffs, no visible bindings at all. The warlock's hands relaxed at his sides. Eyes focused on the back of the head of the pale-faced man in front of him. Clearly, it's his powers holding him in submission. The type of chains that are impossible to break.

"Mr. Pillnick, please tell us who you work for."

His neck twists as he grimaces. His only way of combating the order. He fights long and hard, sweat coating his brow and underarms, spreading as he continues to keep the words trapped behind his dry lips.

"If you will not talk, then we shall bleed your secrets from you."

With a wave of her hand, my mother calls for the man who questioned her. As he passes me, those black pupils widen, taking over the whites of his eyes, before shifting to a crystal blue so clear and vibrant they resemble sheets of ice. His fangs elongate, stabbing into the flesh along the column of the prisoner's neck, his scream vibrating through the room.

The slurp of blood being drunk from the prisoner quiets the room. The sharp metal tang — one I know so well from years of crime scenes and my own kills — permeates the space. A scent that never churned my stomach before, but does now. As his fangs slip free of their puncture wounds, the man's eyes roll back into his head, before his body crumbles to the ground, Bronson's binding magic no longer holding him upright.

"I have the answers we need," he announces, flicking his tongue to the corner of his mouth to clear the spot of blood smeared there.

"Council, please follow me to our meeting room." My mother orders her fellow leaders, followed by hushed words filtering through the room.

Like school children, a line follows Syriah single file, the vampire locking eyes with me as he passes. Those creepy orbs still glow brightly as if he's still hungry for more, sending a chill down my spine.

I'm startled by Oliver's hand on my shoulder. His gaze apologetic. He leads me out of the room and into another sequestered behind yet another wall. It's clearly a walkthrough with a door directly across from us leading to somewhere deep within the house. *How big is this place?*

"Why didn't you speak up?"

"About?" I'm confused about what I was supposed to say. What exactly was I going to contribute when everyone in the room oozed with the desire to rip me apart limb from limb? My mother made it clear I was a hitwoman, Adrian as my mark. Was that not enough? Did that not draw enough unwanted attention my way?

"The list. You had to have known."

I shouldn't be offended. Although Oliver has treated me with kindness and never with disdain, he harbors the same feelings as our kind. For the first time, it's clear in his eyes.

"Sal gives me one name at a time. I don't get a list. I've never had one." My words are a low growl. A warning. I shouldn't feel betrayed, but I do. To have Oliver look at me the way he did guts me.

"I'm sorry. I just... this is a lot. We have kept the phoenixes safe for a long time and then the attempt on your parents. Add you to the mix with Adrian." He shrugs, eyes downcast. "I had to ask."

I understand. I would be cautious of Ari Luxembohrg — no, James — too.

"It's fine." I brush it off.

I've got one foot toward the door when Oliver pulls me back. His large hand clasps at the back of my head. Our eyes lock, breathing ragged but synchronized just before his lips brush mine. A question. My answer is pulling him closer, consuming the taste of him like a starving woman. I wait for the butterflies to come. My insides to heat, but nothing happens as our lips dance against one another. That's not true for him, though, as his length hardens between us. Logically, I want nothing more than to want him. But my body refuses to follow.

The slam of the door against the wall draws us apart. Adrian's venomous stare and heaving chest to greet us.

"What the fuck are you doing?" His words directed solely at Oliver. As if I'm not even in the room.

In an instant Oliver's eyes go wide, pushing me away as if my touch burned him.

"What the hell?"

"I'm — I'm sorry," he stammers, making his way to the door at his back. "I didn't know." He throws a few more apologies before closing the door behind him. Leaving me alone with dark and stormy.

"What was that?" My hand gestures for the door before slapping against my thigh. "Are you that pathetic that you have to ruin everything for me? Why can't you leave me alone?"

I'm so frustrated I want to scream. Want to tear at my hair. All Adrian does is make my life miserable. Yet the burn in my belly I wanted with Oliver comes when I look at him. I stamp it down. I'll never want this pretentious asshole. He can burn in hell for all he puts me through. For the way he talks to me.

"It's law not to put your hands on another's Pair unless it's announced a Pairing won't happen."

I pause.

Shit. Shit. Shit.

I knew it was too good to be true. Things were too easy for me to catch a break with Oliver. Of course he has a Pair. Someone he should love instead of me. Continue the bloodlines and all that. Shame fills me. I may be reckless with my sexual activity, but I'm not a homewrecker. I'll apologize the first chance I get.

"I didn't know he..." I can't finish the sentence.

"Not him. *You*," Adrian growls before leaving the room the door slamming behind him.

Me?

Eighteen

The snow falls in thick flakes as I make my way into the lobby of Salvatore's building. My heart pounds in my chest. I don't want to do this.

The prep needed was grueling. After the council met I was called in. A rare occurrence. Even Adrian stated he's only been called into a council meeting a few times throughout his stint as Second.

They shared the list with me. The names were no surprise. Many have been on my radar for years. The mix of humans and paranormals nearly even. The council members filled me with information to feed to Salvatore.

I'll have to be convincing. No room for hesitation. Knowing now that Salvatore is a warlock, with power nearly rivaling my father's, the stakes are higher. The room to slip up, greater.

I'm escorted to the elevator, a customary procedure for Sal's visitors. The immaculate modern finishes scream of the wealth that lives in this building. Sal pays me well, but whereas those that live here pay cash, I'd be paying a mortgage. Just the same, the level of extravagance here is of no interest to me.

The elevator makes its quick, quiet climb to the penthouse suite atop the building. Floor ninety. Why would someone want to be this high up? There are only two escape options: the elevator and a hidden stairwell on the main level. Knowing Sal's truth, maybe he's not worried because he has flight abilities or some other random magic I know nothing about.

Mundane thoughts swirl through my consciousness. The insignificant things that cross my mind, but never deserve analysis. I only allow it now as a distraction from what I'm about to do. From the lies I am about to tell. Close enough to the truth that only a microscope could prove them irrefutably false.

As the doors slide open, I'm greeted by two security guards. Ones I usually see around, but not in his home. Everything about tonight feels off. Wrong. If it's a trap, I may make it out. My chances higher with Adrian, Tuck, Talia, Bronson, and a wolf-shifter named Lucas all crouched on the roof, waiting for any sign of distress from me.

Passing the guards, their scents permeate the air. Recognition of the twin werewolves now at my back. Guard dogs primed for attack.

"Ahhh, Ari. You've arrived."

Sal comes traipsing from the back of the condo with a goblet of wine in hand. He shimmers in the recessed lighting clad in a silk, gold suit with matching slippers. Usually, he's less ostentatious.

One more detail that's not right. I will my breathing to slow. A silent prayer on repeat for the contents of my stomach not to make a sudden reappearance.

Keep it together, Ari.

"Drink?" he asks, swishing his hips to music only he can hear in his head. His pupils are pinpoints. He's taken something, but who knows what. Sal has never been secretive about the wild array of drugs he drowns his body in.

"Of course." If he's changing the course of our normal meetings, I will do the same. I don't take drinks at Sal's home. Business and pleasure don't mix. It's not a good look. "A bottle of beer, if you have it."

He pauses, his rear facing me, slowly turning to smirk my way. "If I was going to poison you, it wouldn't matter what the drink comes in."

With that, he continues toward the kitchen area just around the corner and returns with a tumbler more than half full of dark amber liquid. "It's your favorite."

He hands it to me, followed by my tentative sip. Flagging me to sit, I do as he asks. Planted in the decorative chair across from where he sprawls on the table, one leg crossed overtop the other, I breathe even to keep my calm.

"Now, why don't you tell me how long you've been on to me?" he grins.

I pause my drink mid-air, ready to take another sip in hopes it steadies my nerves. *Fuck, this is bad. So, so bad.*

"I found out right after you assigned Adrian Alexander to me."

A knowing smirk. "It sure took you long enough to figure it out."

"So, can I assume you've known what I am since we met?"

"You're a smart one. That's why I picked you. It also helped that you're an orphan and had no ties to our world. That much easier to make you kill your own kind."

Flames flare beneath the barrier of my skin, my blood boiling. I'm pissed that Salvatore thought he could use me as an unknowing pawn in his game. I'm even angrier at myself for having to be told I was nothing more than that. That I couldn't see the signs for myself. Sal will pay. For the heartache and the attempt on my parents.

"I guess you still are, with your parents out of the picture." He takes a long gulp of his wine. "I am sorry about that." A smug note to his words.

I'm not an orphan. I never was.

"I didn't know them. It means nothing to me." My chin lifts a little higher. A show of nonchalance, even though my insides shatter at speaking that lie. Yet another pain point I will make him and his followers pay for.

"You have information for me, then?"

"I do."

I tell him everything. A word-for-word recount of the script I was handed. Only pausing when he asks questions. The dull tap of a finger on a tablet screen stills for a moment, the dog behind me grunting at my responses. I assume the conversation is being recorded as well, both audio and visual.

Fine by me. Let them search. Let them try to come for us. We're ready this time.

It takes me nearly an hour to get through it all, taking one last gulp of my bourbon, sporting my shit-eating grin.

"That's everything."

"Yes, well, thank you. Quite informative." The twitch of his brow makes me cross my legs to hide the shifting in my seat. *Is he doubting me?*

Eager to remove myself from Sal's sanctuary, I turn for the exit.

"One more thing," he calls after me, stopping me in my tracks. "Since Adrian is clearly out of the question for you now, I guess I'll need to hire someone else to dispatch of him." Not a question, but a statement.

A chill steals down my spine, mixing with the sweat pooling at my lower back. He knows I won't kill Adrian. Yet, there's one last card to play. "Salvatore, I am still in your employ. You choose what needs to be done."

A full smile spreads on his face. A sight so rare, bile rises up my throat. "Yes, I'll have someone else take care of him. Wouldn't want to break your little *bird* heart."

Falling for the bait, I bite. "Why would killing Adrian Alexander break my heart?"

A terrifying cackle escapes Sal before he slaps his thigh, heading into the heart of the condo. "You should ask him. Come back to me if his answer doesn't align with what I said."

The guards shuffle me to the elevator, the doors closing to the sound of Salvatore's boisterous laughter.

Nineteen

The knotting of my intestines steals my attention as I slide into the nondescript SUV beside Adrian. The weight of their stares nearly makes me look up. Sal's words crawling over one another in my head. I'm incensed by his insinuation that I couldn't do what needs to be done. There's nothing about Adrian that would make me change my mind about killing him if that was what I was still resigned to do. Not even being of my bloodline could stop me.

"Are you going to fill us in?" Tuck calls from the front passenger seat.

I hesitate, deciding what to tell them. It seemed as though Sal consumed what I fed him. That hunger in his eyes and that telling smirk pulling at the corner of his mouth as I relayed the truth I wanted him to hear.

What he said about me murdering Adrian doesn't add up, though. I have no deep-set feelings for him, only loyalty to my family. To my kind. If he disappeared, I would go about my life, not being taunted by him. Not wanting to crawl out of my skin because once again he gained the upper hand.

I can tell myself that story. Feed it to the pit of darkness deep inside me, but a small part of me knows it's not the truth. Knows that on some level I would miss Adrian and his broody stare. Or his ability to ruin any bit of fun or happiness for me. The way his eyebrow quirks, nearly touching that one tendril of hair that sometimes breaks free while we argue. What I would miss most, the way he looked at me when he caught Oliver and me tangled in the dim lights of that room. The way he sent him away and confessed what a betrayal it was to kiss someone else's Pair. Almost as if he was happy and angry, all at once there's someone out there just for me.

I tell the only truth my friends need to hear with a deep exhale. "Salvatore knows I won't kill Adrian. He's sending someone else."

If he could slide any further away from me, he would. Curling his enormous frame into the door. I've never seen Adrian show genuine fear. Never coiling into himself at the prospect of him being the next paranormal to meet their maker. No, Adrian Alexander, stands tall against it. Ignores it.

The rest of the drive back to the safe house was quiet. The residents of the upscale suburb had long since returned home and sequestered themselves indoors.

Hand poised on the handle of the door, Adrian's fingers wrap around my opposite wrist. "Walk with me." I give him a nod before hopping down to the curb.

Tuck remains, glare snapping between the two of us. That brotherly protectiveness radiating off him in waves. Before Adrian pulls me behind him, Tuck stops him, hand on his shoulder. "Tell. Her."

The words a whispered command. Not meant for me to hear. A warning from my brother to our Second. A tone only Tuck or my parents could get away with. I don't miss the shifting of Adrian's eyes from Tuck's face to mine. Or the way his muscles tense and shoulders rise to nearly touch the lobe of his ear. The press of his lips into a straight line. Resignation. A fight for defiance, but acceptance, too.

Tuck releases him, quick strides carrying him to the front door, where Talia waits. Adrian's grip on my hand doesn't loosen as we huddle through the cold and wind. He leads me around the side of the house, through the yard, and down to the beachfront at the very edge of the property.

"Are you going to tell me what Sal actually said to you about me?"

I ponder this for a long time. Knowing any rendition of bringing the words to life will sound ridiculous. "He said it would break my heart to kill you. That I should ask you why." His grip on my fingers tightens, but his focus remains on the crash of dark waves ahead. Lake Michigan becomes quite brutal with the wind, but it's my favorite scent, sound, and sight of all.

He's quiet next to me. Long enough that I'm convinced no answer will come, my mouth opening to speak, just as his lips collide with mine.

His warmth envelopes me, powerful arms pulling me close. His very presence consumes me, like the flames that I often let soar over my body when too much has bottled up inside. As his tongue slips across the seam of my lips, I let him in. The taste of him is one I don't think I could ever get enough of. Ever replace.

Oliver's kiss comes unbidden to my mind. His and every other man before. They've never felt like this. Their bodies never fit with mine the way Adrian does. His very presence like the air I need to breathe. The skies I need to soar through.

Just as suddenly as his lips found mine, he pulls away but keeps me close. Our foreheads pressed firmly together. I have more questions. I need more answers, but I can't breathe. The air won't flow into my lungs and back out as it should. That is what Adrian does to me. I've tried so hard to ignore it. To pretend I feel nothing for him other than disdain. But it's a lie. I knew that when Sal looked me in the eye, vowing to send someone else to take this man's life. To take him from me. Someone who isn't mine to have.

"Are you going to tell me?" I whisper. His fingers knot in the wool of my overcoat just below my waist.

"Do you remember when I told you that you had a Pair?"

I nod. Our foreheads still pressed firmly together. Those bright eyes of his now wide-open focused on me. They've always been vivid, piercing orbs of green. Vibrant. But tonight it's almost as if they are glowing. As if a neon light shines behind them.

"It's okay, Adrian. I know we never see eye to eye. I know we hate—" He cuts off my words, his mouth molding to mine, before quickly pulling away.

"I could never hate you, Ari James. Not even if I tried. Not even if I wanted to. You're my Pair."

His words drift into the space surrounding us, a warm blanket making my heart stop.

My Pair.

Twenty

I do my best to avoid the safe house and Adrian for the next week. I may have admitted I want him — to myself. His truth about us being paired was a surprise, though now obvious. A small truth cradled in my hands with a question mark, so much heavier than the feathers I keep tucked in my worn leather jacket. I don't know how to handle it or accept it or deny it. Trying to fathom what I might actually want — to claim it for myself, absurd.

"Yo, Luxe," one of the burly cops next in line to make detective calls to me as I hustle down the hall, lost in my own thoughts. "That case you solved earlier this week. Seemed like a long shot. If you, uh, have some time..." He absentmindedly adjusts his gun belt. A nervous tic. "I would love to talk about what you saw. You know, what the rest of us missed?"

There's a genuine interest driving the upturn of his mouth. Many of the men pretend that I just get lucky. That I don't have actual skill as a homicide detective. That all I have to offer is my pretty face and the sway of my hips to get people to talk to me.

Few take me as seriously as Chief Barlow and Gomez. This guy, Johnny — I think that's his name — definitely does. This is the first time he has asked me to review a dicier case, though.

"I'll meet you at the bar at seven. Have my drink ready." He flashes another wide smile before disappearing in the opposite direction. The decent ones like him make my love of what I do that much more important. Their acknowledgments make it that much more worth it.

"Ari, you ready to head out?" Gomez is perched on the side of my desk, his thick hair disheveled and damp.

"You look like a wet dog." Laughter bubbles around us. The guys making a show of me picking on Gomez. Typical. Truth is, I don't think I would survive this job without having him as my partner.

"Let's go." I grab my coat, balancing my coffee in one hand, wallet in the other, and keys between my teeth.

We're back on the James case today. No matter how many of our leads run cold, we're thrown back in with a new one. Our resolve to solve the case never wavers. Deep down, I know we won't get anywhere. I doubt we'll find who actually did this. Not for lack of trying or wanting that justice. Sal had someone try to murder my family and I want them dead.

Just two days ago, I was allowed to see my dad again. His body long ago sewn closed. The stitches faded and his skin healed. Bronson left me alone with him for hours, while I kept my ear to his cotton-covered chest, my eyes pressing shut with each heartbeat. He's still alive, suspended in time.

Bronson explained the magic that he had to have in his system. A custom potion to suspend life. Unfortunately, the magic needed to pull him back out is rare, and Bronson doesn't know it.

So I stayed there, ear-to-chest, and listened to his heartbeat so sedate I convinced myself I wouldn't hear it again. Fear that I wouldn't be able to help and I'd be powerless, overwhelmed me. My only chance to meet the man I've been longing to know my entire life, vaporized.

The lead we're following today is a former informant for the PD. His life of varied crimes and substance abuse, the anvil that we can dangle over his head to make him cooperate. A laundry list of charges we could still arrest him for should he go against us.

Lamont Wills looks all of his forty years and then some. The graying strands through his thick dark beard, the ashen gray of his skin that should still be taught, sagging from the years of drugs polluting his system, coupled with the stints in prison and rehab.

"Lamont," I call his name as we pull into the alley where we know he loiters most afternoons.

"Gorgeous," he coos, a smile creasing my face. He may not be the type of company I would normally keep, but his jolly spirit still always lifts mine.

"Language," Gomez chides as he slams the car door behind him. Lamont's hands lift in a placating gesture before throwing me a wink.

"Tell me what you've got for me."

I slump onto the hood of the car, focusing solely on Lamont's face. Knowing Gomez won't take his focus off his hands. Lamont's always behaved, knowing his place in the world now. If they're not careful, the eyes will give them away. His hard years have worn on him; every emotion, every thought broadcasted on a big screen for my viewing pleasure. Perfect for me.

"There's a guy, Rolan. I don't know no last name. Dresses real suave-like. Shiny shoes. He was fucking with the ladies around here, bragging about all the people he been killing."

My teeth grind. Sal is getting sloppy. If this was one of his guys, he would be quite unhappy to hear he's running his mouth around town, even if they were just prostitutes. "He's a regular?"

"The last few months, yeah. Comes like clockwork. Every Friday night."

I nod in thanks, throw Lamont a hundred-dollar bill, and get back behind the wheel. Peeling out of the alley, I'm seething. The heat radiating from my body, making the air flowing through the vents nearly suffocate me.

"I know what you're thinking, and the answer is no."

Gomez knows me better than I wish he did. His intuition regarding my thoughts, irritating at best. A partnership that allows him to see right through me. No, never mind. He can't stop someone like me. Never could. Not a chance.

Twenty-One

Johnny's seated at the bar, his stool guarding the one in the corner I claimed as my own. It's embarrassing how predictable I've become over the years. The realization slapping me in the face with Adrian upending my life.

My phone was a non-stop vibration in my pocket on my walk here. Adrian clearly thought if he kept calling it would make me answer. I'm not ready to face *him* or *us* or *this*. It was hard enough showing up at his house on Mom's orders two nights ago, just to chicken out when he took too long to answer the door.

Otherwise, complete and total avoidance. You would think my tactics would have sent the message. Not for Adrian. A man who always gets what he wants. The question is, does he actually want me or is it just this pair thing keeping him attached?

"Hey Johnny," I pat his back as I round behind him, my other hand grabbing for my drink.

I've barely taken my first gulp before he dives right in. His analysis of the case rolls off his tongue as if practiced. The evidence he thought crucial and the pieces he knew I called out that everyone else didn't. I don't have to say much as he rifles through it all from memory, only referencing notes on his phone a few times when he's trying to remember specific dates or numbers. I'm thoroughly impressed by his preparation, nodding along with his assessment.

Once I've given him mine, the conversation drifts from work to funny stories about him growing up. How different he and his brothers are. His poor mother birthed six of them, each wildly distinct from the last.

It's nice to just sit and talk to someone. To not have the weight of two worlds on my shoulders for just a little while. Then I see him. His looming form filling the doorway, nostrils flared like a raging bull's.

Quick, long strides carry him toward me, all the light-hearted energy that had been billowing through me dissipates. Johnny doesn't notice, regaling about the time his brothers decided they were going to make water slides off the roof of their house.

"Is your phone suddenly not working?" Adrian breathes, the calm coating his words hiding the searing rage beneath. The bulging of his veins at his throat and across the backs of his hands gave it away. It's only as his fingers grip my biceps, pulling me to my feet, that Johnny steps in, attempting to block Adrian from me.

"My phone is fine." I jerk away from him, only causing myself more pain as his grip tightens.

"When I call, you answer. When I text, you better fucking answer." His words growled in my face. His jaw tight, lips pressed firmly together, but it's his eyes that hold his truth. The same anger doesn't live there; fear does. That glow that I swore I saw the other night, flashing.

"Adrian." My voice is soft. My touch even softer. "Tell me what's going on?"

"Ari?" Johnny questions, clearly not understanding what's happening here.

"It's fine, Johnny." My brain freezes, searching for a way to explain this man's hands on me. To explain his temper and his frustration directed only at me. "My." Gulp. "... boyfriend."

His glare darkens. His gaze drifting from Adrian's hand wrapped around my arm to his face.

"I don't care who he is." He squares up with Adrian as he says his peace. "You don't put your hands on a woman like that! Especially a cop."

Glowing emeralds never leave mine as he responds, "With all due respect, *kid*. You have no place telling me a damn thing. Ari, let's go."

With a small smile in Johnny's direction, I follow Adrian from the bar, down the block, and around the corner to his parked car. The moment the doors close, I'm in his face. The release of my anger and embarrassment a roaring assault. He takes it all. Something like shame shadowing his features.

"I was scared something happened to you."

"Scared?" The shock clear in my tone. "Of what?"

He tells me everything. The attack on the safe house. The message filtered out through the paranormal phone tree. Ten more bodies, various species sprawled out for anyone to find in the park. My fury cools as he pulls out onto the Chicago streets, navigating to an even more distant suburb I've never been to.

The sprawling land surrounding this house compliments the grandeur of the estate. The gap between residences so vast, a car is the only practical way to reach your neighbor's driveway. A couple of dozen cars line the street and triple that along the mile-long drive. Adrian leads the car through the wood line to the garage. The door well-placed at the side of the monstrosity.

There are bodies everywhere. Not just my kind, but all. I don't think I can sense emotions, but every bit of space is crowded with a mixture of them. Tumbling over each other, overwhelming my own ability to keep calm. Adrian pulls me close, shoving us through the throng until we find my mother in what must be a family room. Relief seeps into her features as she sees me, pulling me away from Adrian and into her embrace.

"What's going on... Mom?"

I'd started using the term shortly after we met but still hesitate from time to time. It has never been a question of loving her. She's my mother. It's openly stating who she is that's hard. Voicing that single word still gives me pause.

"We'll explain everything soon." Her finger brushes my cheek before Adrian's arm is around me once more. "Give him a chance." She gives a small smile before being approached by a squat man, his nose pinched and angled like a goblin. I'm wondering if those exist, too.

"Luxe," a familiar voice bellows over the chorus of chatter. I turn to find Gomez coming toward me, his wife and children in tow. "Shit, I'm glad he found you."

Found me. What the hell is going on? Why is my partner here?

"Care to tell me why you're here?"

He smiles like he always does. That knowing look he gives me. "I thought for sure you'd have figured it out by now."

Searching my mind, I try to find the answers when it hits me.

"All this time... You're a werewolf."

His grin widens, showcasing canines I always thought were unnaturally large. "Wolf-shifter, actually." He shrugs. "Someone had to keep an eye on you."

"Have you known this whole time? Everything?"

He shakes his head, taking his baby girl from his wife. "The Salvatore part was news to me. I knew what you were when we met. Why do you think I requested to be your partner?"

Adrian grabs the little girl, her stubby arms reaching for him. Her tiny body even smaller against his. A lopsided, toothy grin spreads and her small chubby hands pull at his cheeks. "Thank you for always keeping her safe," he mumbles, his words garbled as those same little fingers pinch his lips together.

Gomez nods before pulling the little girl back to his hip.

"Everyone, I need your attention."

FEATHERS OF TRUTH

My mother may be a small woman, but nothing but quiet breaths fill the room as we all heed her command. A longing pulls at my chest. A need to make her proud. To learn from her. To be just like her someday.

Twenty-Two

The leaders gather behind my mother. Just as they had the last time we'd brought our different species together. Just as before, Syriah James stands just a hair's breadth ahead of them. I would expect the way we've gathered here, they would all stand in line together. But the formation says something more. My mother is the one they stand behind.

Pride and dread mix in my chest. It's an inspiring display. The way they look to the woman who birthed me for guidance, protection, and direction. Yet not understanding this small power move reminds me just how much I don't know and understand about our world. I'm in the dark despite being thrown in head-first months ago.

"Salvatore Danarius has declared war on all those who stand against him. He has matching numbers in his shadow, for those we have on our side. They have no boundaries, no cares for breaking the laws that govern our kind. We'll need to be prepared to loosen the reins we've confined ourselves to. It's the only way to ensure those of you in this room survive and support of our leadership remains in the end. Anyone who walks out of this room in opposition or betrays us in any way will be executed with prejudice."

There's no hesitation in my mother's words. The meaning permeates through the pores in our skin. Captivating us. Binding us to her without a second thought. Young, old, male, female, every eye stays focused only on her. No flinches, no outward signs of rebellion.

I flinch, though. Recoiling at her words. I shouldn't. For all the lives I've taken without remorse, without caring what it meant to anyone but Salvatore. I should be comfortable with the brutality, but I'm not. Somewhere along the way — finding my people — killing them became the one thing I'm not willing to do.

Listening to my mother continue her rallying speech, I know I will have to find the Ari I'd been before. It's clear some of us will die. Some of us will get cold feet and run to whoever is winning the war. Just as the thought clutches at my consciousness, my mother's navy blue eyes find mine. The same glow I've seen in Adrian's shines in hers. The flecks of silver a near clone to my own, bright and glaring.

Her piercing stare tells me everything. *It's time to stand tall, Ari.* It will be me fighting at her side. Leaving the mercy I've only recently found behind me once more.

"Tell us, where will we send those that can't fight?" A high-pitched male voice from the rear of the room calls. The quiver in his words revealing his fear to the entire room.

A man I've not seen before steps forward, a mesmerizing appeal to him. The lilt of his words draws me in, the comprehension of what he's saying not computing. Many of the others in the room lean into his enchantment as our bodies angle toward him. I can't explain it. Can't resist the pull to go to him.

A hand on my wrist holds me where I am. Adrian's grip keeping me at his side as if he knows, but can resist whatever it is drawing me forward. I don't fight it, as he laces his fingers through mine, my focus solely on the magical voice drifting over us all.

His plan is simple. Those needing to remain out of harm's way will be safe. Gomez's daughter whimpers behind me. So young and innocent. I assume they don't have control of their wolves yet. Their lack of being one with their wolves doing nothing to give them the protection they might need. Yet, behind their eyes lies the truth. They understand war.

Fear-driven questions are thrown at my mother and her counterpart. Fractions of the crowd listen intently, others begin conversations amongst themselves. Leaning in close to Adrian, inhaling his scent as I do, I ask what's been plaguing me. "Why is my mother speaking for everyone?"

His jaw twitches. Those muscles flaring to life the way they often do when I've asked him a question that wears on his nerves. He doesn't answer me as he grabs me by my arm, threatening to leave bruises along with the ones from earlier tonight. He throws a nod to someone to my right, our movement just quick enough that I don't see who it is.

Anxiety and anger roar from the crowd around us as we shove through. A door appears, seemingly out of nowhere. Adrian pulling it wide and shoving me down the stairs with a yelp. Heavy steps follow me. Two sets of them.

Adrian guides me through the dark before a light flickers to life. The fluorescent glow stings my eyes, despite only being in the dark for mere minutes. My frustration grows as I lock eyes with the three men in the room alongside me. Adrian is beyond pissed, his arms crossed at his chest and legs spread shoulder-width apart at my side. Tuck looks like he's about to shit himself and Oliver just flat-out confused.

"Someone better start talking. I'm tired of always being in the dark about something between you three."

"Well, Tucker," Adrian snarls. His glare pointed solely at my brother. "Care to tell me why Ari is asking me why *her* mother is speaking for everyone?"

Tuck shuffles from foot to foot. His eyes stay trained on the floor, the uncomfortable shifting of his feet adding to the tension in the room. More truths kept from me.

"And you, *Training Officer*," Oliver's title thrown at him as a mockery. A clear lack of respect for how he's performed his duties. "You never mentioned how the hierarchy of our world works during those training sessions? Just didn't come up?" A shrug of his heavy shoulders.

Oliver's Adam's apple bobs before Tuck finally opens his mouth to speak. "Ari, well we are, um." Stuttering hesitance is a look I've never seen on my brother, one I am not accustomed to dealing with. Although we've gotten to know each other well, he's still practically a stranger. I recall my mom's fierce look, so I dig deep for old Ari and demand answers the way I always would have.

Charging forward, my hand pushes into Tuck's chest, backing him against the nearest pillar. "Talk," I grit through my teeth, baring them. The flames flicker beneath the surface, threatening to break free, but I hold them at bay.

"There's a hierarchy," Tuck begins. He goes through the structure. Regional, state, country, worldwide. The endless grappling for the balance of power that goes into creating each council. Constant scrutiny of the laws that bind us all, always at the forefront. Then he drops the bomb on me, the one I should have known. Something I should have understood long ago.

"Since before many of us can remember, there's one true ruler. Head, leader, whatever term you want to use for all paranormals. A phoenix. Always a phoenix."

I can't breathe. The pieces come together in surprising clarity. Why it was such a problem for my parents to pair and wed. Why we have the protections we do. The wide birth everyone gives me. The respect my mother has from just breathing. How they all follow her blindly without a second thought, regardless of species.

"Our parents preside over every paranormal..." It's not a question as my eyes close, the weight of the truth sinking in. I'm not an anxious person. Not easily overwhelmed. I rarely give in to my emotions like others do. I'm rational. Detached. A bit of a daredevil. But I'm done.

I wanted to be part of it. This is just too much, too fast.

Pushing Tuck aside, I'm trudging up the stairs. Even my name on Adrian's lips doesn't make me look back. Not this time.

I pause at the top step. Hand poised on the doorknob. My last words drifting down into the space below me. "I can't do this. I can't continue to be kept in the dark and live amongst you like it's all fine."

They don't stop me as I leave the house. I have no car here. No way to get back to *my* home. I'm not even entirely sure where we are, so I just start walking. Letting the click of my heeled boots scrape against the concrete. When they finally ache, my feet swelling within my leather footwear, I finally call for an Uber, standing on the side of the road, alone.

The ride back to the city is filled with me fighting back tears and mentally beating myself up for not asking more questions. For not noticing more of the details. But I'm even angrier at myself for allowing them to sweep me so far into this world, while giving me so little.

I have no doubt they will come after me. Likely Adrian and Tuck as a duo. But I don't want to see them right now. I can't. I need to think. Maybe wallow a little, too.

The need to keep space from them is my only concern. My apartment isn't an option. The beach is my only place of solace.

Ass planted in the freezing cold sand, with the wind whipping across Lake Michigan stinging my skin, I stare out into the darkness. Tears I haven't shed in over a decade finally fall. I'm not alone anymore, but I'm just as lonely as I've always been.

Twenty-Three

I don't rise until the sun does, finally making my way back to my apartment. My feet throb and my heart hurts, but I make it back in record time. The receptionist who always sits at the front for day shift eyeing me warily as I enter my building. She knows this look. I've had it for years as I've worked cases through the night only to return in the morning an extremely haggard version of myself.

The moment my apartment door clicks shut, I allow my frustrated groan to break free. Exhaustion pulls at my limbs, slowing my thoughts and movements, as I remove my clothes, piece by piece. A sudden cough stops me as I unbutton my slacks, fingers frozen mid-maneuver.

The frantic racing of my heart nearly knocks me into the far wall, my body instantly alight with flames. Even as a child, I could always control them. When I wanted to see how long it would take for my skin to burn, I called for the blazing inferno. I never had to master that control. Yet, my intruder destroyed that leash I never had to hold tight to.

Only when my mother rounds the corner into the entryway, her face revealing she is no threat to me, do the flames stop arching for my ceiling. They keep close to my now exposed skin, desperate to flicker with life until my heart rate slows.

My eyes widen realizing there's nothing left to cover me. My clothing burnt to gray ash at my feet.

Perfectly shaped brows rise toward her straight bangs. Her petite mouth caught in an O. Likely, not from my nakedness, but the raging flames that nearly burned the place to the ground. Blackened hardwood floors beneath my feet that will need to be replaced yet again.

It takes nearly twenty minutes of concentration for them to fade completely. Deep breaths and closed eyes. All the shit they teach you in meditation to center yourself. Something Gomez insisted I needed for my raging temper actually coming in handy for the first time. As my lids peel open, ready to face the woman who birthed me once more, a final stuttering breath escapes me.

"Have you always been able to do that?" she asks, her inflection skeptical. Questioning, as if it's not common to spontaneously ignite on a Tuesday. Like every phoenix doesn't crackle with licking flames of chaos.

"Since I first called on my phoenix," I admit.

She nods but makes no move to come toward me. Taking that as my one chance to escape, I slip down the hall into the comfort of my bedroom.

FEATHERS OF TRUTH

Sunlight beams brightly through the floor-to-ceiling windows. Its warmth staunching the chill that sunk into my bones from my night by the water. Once dressed, I join her again, nestling into the couch across from her.

The little girl in me curls in on herself. Legs crisscrossed, despite my knees begging me to choose any other position, a pillow nestled in my lap, so I have something to hold on to. A shield I'd never need with Syriah, but comforts me just the same.

"Why are you staring at me like that?"

"Curiosity." Her soothing voice drifts over me as it often does when we have these moments alone. I wish I had more of them. If our time together is short-lived, I want to keep the little pieces of her. When you've lost everything, you learn to grasp onto the little bits that are most precious when you can.

Pulling the oversize sleeves of my sweatshirt over my hands — mostly to hide the tremble — I wait for her to say more. The silence stretching between us seemingly endless.

"Why?" I whisper.

"Fire magic isn't common."

Without thinking, my head tilts to the side, taking in her statement. *Fire magic.* It never occurred to me the flames weren't part of being a phoenix. The commissioned art in the texts always shows the birds in flames. Although, they're referenced at times of rebirth. Why would I think we could summon that gift anytime like we could our inner birds?

"Can you?"

She shakes her head, a small smile pulling at the corners of her lips. "Your father has fire magic. Rare these days, but it was the dominant element of his bloodline. When we first met, he set himself on fire, thinking it would impress me." A distant chuckle bubbles past her lips as she fiddles with the thin chain of the necklace I'd noticed before, but never asked about. Her eyes drift as she gets lost in the memory of her and him. Love shining bright behind them.

I want that someday.

"I figured we all caught on fire at will." The statement sounds ridiculous as I say it out loud.

She's quick to come sit next to me, pulling me into her side. I let her, needing the physical contact. The desire for someone else's touch usually found in the beds of random men. A pastime no longer existent since diving into my double life. No time. No energy. No interest.

"Mom," the term finally slipping from me with ease. Her hum in response, chin pressed to the top of my head, is reassuring, encouraging me to go on. "Did you know Adrian was my Pair?"

"I did. Likely before he did."

"What if I'm not sure I want him?"

My voice is small. That little girl staying present. The teenager who wanted her mother there to guide her through those days of liking boys driving the knotting of my hands in my lap. The many questions I would have asked. *What do I do? How do I act? How will I know?* Whitney Houston's lyrics playing on repeat in my head.

A burly laugh vibrates from her chest. A laugh she's never shared with me, but I secretly love. "Oh sweetheart, if you even remotely thought that was the truth, you wouldn't be asking me." Her hand smooths the wild waves from my face. "We have more important things to discuss."

I sit up, looking directly into her matching eyes. The color I've studied for years. Memorizing every nuance, so when I saw their match, I would know it instantly. I would know who my family was.

"I should have been the one to tell you how important our family is. It should never have been something I allowed someone else to do for me. I didn't want to push you. You and Tucker had already formed such a bond. I thought it would be easier coming from him." Her hand brushes my cheek and under my chin.

"Now you know, though. As a Phoenix, they chose us to lead. When a phoenix dies, a new one must take their place."

"We don't die though." Confusion clear in my tone. I'd studied it. Searched every book, every website. Consulted every expert. I mean, we die — eventually — but not at random.

"We do. Mythology is just that. The tales of our kind are mostly true. We have two ways to die. Choice and penetration with a very specific metal. It nulls our regeneration powers. Instead of being reborn from the ashes, the ashes will be all that remains if the rebirth process begins." Choice is the version printed in the tomes of textbooks lining my shelf.

My eyes close. The gun Salvatore gifted me. Equipped with bullets only he could supply. He'd always told me to use that when in doubt. For the times when "usual" methods for murder didn't do the trick. Now I understand why.

"Is it the same effect on other supernaturals?"

"Absolutely." She gives a small twitch of a smile before frowning. "For most, death comes as easy as it would for a human."

It all makes so much sense. The privilege of having a Phoenix rule our world of make-believe. Why others look to us. We're nearly invincible. The closest thing to true immortality. A way to ensure continuity through centuries. My brain aches with the sheer amount of information I've gathered these past few months. My world ruthlessly turned upside down.

A knock at the door steals the moment. "Ah, breakfast." My mother laughs, driving her small fists into the cushions to hoist herself from the sofa. She reemerges, balancing several bags with the Yolk logo and multiple drinks. "Now, I know you like to eat the way I do, so let's dig in while I answer any questions you have."

That's what we do. Gobbling down bacon, eggs, potatoes, pancakes, coffee, and orange juice. I'm grateful for picking such loose clothing as my belly distends from my indulgent intake of carbs and meat. I'm not a small woman; my mother is. But we just ate enough for six men.

Head resting in her lap, we laugh and talk, her fingers combing through my tangled strands, the tips brushing against my scalp soothing me.

The loneliness I felt last night abates, a feeling like hope blossoming in my chest. Resolution in my gut. Decidedness in my mind. I may not have known this woman for long, but she is my mother and she loves me.

My counterparts are doing what they can to fight for an undisturbed existence. For happiness. She loves them too. I would do anything she asked of me to protect that. To keep her and Tuck and my dad safe. To protect Adrian.

He's weaseled his way into my heart. I may accept the truth in our bond, but I don't know how to make that commitment to him. I have never made any sort of emotional pledge to anyone but Gomez and me. Gomez, so he makes it home to his beautiful family every night and for me to be the strongest woman alive. How do I give the man that makes me see red another piece of myself?

A tomorrow problem if I ever heard one.

Twenty-Four

By the time I wake, the living room is draped in darkness. My tired body still curled into a protective ball. At some point my mother left, leaving me in the exact spot I fell asleep in. A sticky note on the coffee table explains it all. Her need to return to one of the safe houses, so she's properly guarded.

I know where she'll go first. Back to my father's side. Like ships passing in the night, we've caught one another coming and going from his room. The sense of longing pulling at her angelic features. I miss him too. A man I've never met.

Stretching with a loud groan, I shuffle to my room in search of my phone. Fortunately, I'd removed it from my pocket when I heard my mom cough earlier, so it didn't burn too. Otherwise, I'd be scraping melted metal from my hardwood floors tonight. Not something I want to do again. It is not cheap replacing three random floorboards.

There are a series of text message notifications. Several from Tuck demanding I call him, along with five missed calls from him.

Straight to voicemail. *He'll get back to me.*

There are a few GIFs from Gomez and the guys. A practice that's become common amongst us detectives. We see such horrible things every day. We all need to lighten the mood sometimes. To remember how to laugh and let go of the tension that coils our shoulders and knots our insides.

I'm surprised there's not a peep from Adrian. I expected his overbearing alpha-hole personality to come shining through after he told me the truth about us. Nothing, though. I need to talk to him. Lay down ground rules for us to operate by. I need time to figure it out. I'd be a liar if I said I'm not overwhelmed with everything. Adding in a fated mate or some shit is more than I can manage. I can definitely do without that cherry on top.

Donning a pair of black skinny jeans, a fitted tee, and a leather jacket, I stalk down to the garage. Normally, I would take a walk. Stretch my legs. The only exercise I ever gave my bird. But tonight there's a tension in the air. The unknown lurks in the shadows. A weight hanging over us all waiting to drop. Hopping into my SUV, I've only just started the ignition when Salvatore's name pops up on the caller ID.

"Hello?" The lone word a question for the first time. After our last encounter, I hadn't expected to hear from him again so soon. I knew in time the taunts would come. The attempts on Adrian's life, too. Something I refuse to let happen. I'm not in love with the asshat by any means, just the same, I can't imagine a world without him. Not anymore.

"I have a job for you."

Ice shards fill my gut. It can't be Adrian he's asking me for. He already knew. Knew, I wouldn't kill him for any amount of money. How he knew the man is my Pair, is beyond me, but I can't afford to underestimate Salvatore.

No, the piercing fear that has me clutching the steering wheel so tight I may pull it from the dash is because I don't want to hear the name of the next paranormal he wants me to murder. My kind, a stepping stone for him to have power that was never his.

"Who?" The faintest quake in my voice. One I hope Sal misses thanks to the car speaker and the rush of the wind from the open window. It's entirely too hot in here and if I catch on fire again, it's going to be a bigger problem than showing Mom my birthday suit this morning.

"The info's been sent. You have five days."

The line goes dead. The tires rotating against the pavement are the only addition to the soundtrack of my erratic breathing. Two months ago, I wouldn't have blinked at a spontaneous call from Salvatore, asking me to murder some unsuspecting someone. I would have quirked a grin at the dollar amount wired to my bank account. The pep in my step so bouncy you'd think I was a kid on Christmas.

Not tonight, though. As I pull to the curb in front of Adrian's corner lot, my heart hurts. Panic floods me. Sadness beckons to pull me under the waves threatening to drown me. How many more will I take out of this world so I can keep living in it without one of Salvatore's bullets through my chest?

I've never questioned an assignment. Not until Adrian. Not until immersing myself into a world I wasn't sure existed.

Cutting the engine, the neighborhood around me is quiet. It's relatively early in the evening. I would expect soccer moms still strolling the block, walking their golden retrievers, kids running in the park, but there is no one around. Most of the houses have lights on. *The Brady Bunch* families never passing the sheer curtains they insist on for decor. The lack of opacity as if they wanted to expose their entire lives to their neighbors' nosy whims. Not me. Blackout curtains only.

Adrian's doorbell chimes like any other. The silence that follows sends a chill up my spine. He should be home. There's nothing going on at the safe houses tonight. I checked my emails before I left. I ring again before my fist raps against the door. A low creak as it drifts open with the second *tap* of my knuckles.

Deep breath.

This is the stuff of movies. The moments we yell at the screen for the actors to run. But I don't run. I've always bolted toward danger. Even when every fiber of my being told me not to. When logic encouraged me to go the other way. Drawing my gun from the holster at my hip, knees bent into a crouch, I push the door open further. My boots make the slightest *clap* against the hardwood floors. Otherwise silence.

Eyes wide, I take in the space. Hurricane Katrina must have swept through. Every inch of fabric is shredded. Every piece of art shorn apart. Table legs splintered as if heavy bodies crashed into them. Floorboards scraped and lunging upward. Boulder-sized holes in the walls, the railing of the stairwell hanging at a precarious angle.

I know better than to call out. To draw attention to someone stumbling upon the scene. I have no idea if I'm here alone. The one thing my phoenix isn't good for. Easing the door closed behind me, the soft click signifying it's in place, I bolt it shut. Yet another dumb move. But if someone else is still here, I want them trapped with me. No easy escape for the criminal I'll steal a last breath from. They won't make it out. I only hope that Adrian wasn't here when this happened. That he is safe.

I don't pray. Not until now. For Adrian. For all of us.

Slowly, I creep my way through the entire main level, only releasing the breath I was holding when I circle back to the entryway. The culprits made a point of destroying as much as possible. No surface or item left untarnished.

Staying along the edge of the stairs closest to the wall, so as not to step on any areas that may creak, I make my way up to the second story.

In movies, cops always keep their guns pointed down. Not me. Mine stays high, left arm extended, and ready to take my shot. I've been in too many situations where those seconds are precious. Moments you won't get back if you lose them. The milliseconds that add up to your death versus theirs.

Much like the downstairs, they left the rooms in complete shambles. I've never been up here, but it's obvious these rooms were decorated similarly to the downstairs. Adrian's delicate balance between modern and historical. There's none of it left now. Only a disaster that will have to be cleaned. Hell, he might have to gut the damn place to get it back to what it once was.

I know I've come to the master bedroom as the scent of him fills my nostrils. What was once a grand king-size bed now topples to its side, as if its legs gave out and couldn't stay standing for another second. Nearly three-quarters up the wall, gashes tear into the paint and drywall. Slashes that could only come from massive claws. Nothing human did that. My throat suddenly goes dry, my gun arm dropping just a fraction for the first time I can remember.

Adrian, where are you?

Just as I back out of the room, confident there's no one left here with me, I'm grabbed from behind. A muscular arm strapped across my stomach, trapping my shooting arm, with the other hand clasped tightly over my mouth. There's no time to scream. No time to react, as I'm dragged backward, disappearing into the wall just outside the bedroom door.

Only once we've slunk so far into the darkness, there's no telling how far we've gone, does the man let me go. My breathing ragged huffs stealing the quiet around us.

A phone flashlight illuminates the empty space between us.

A sob escapes me. Genuine tears break free as I wrap my arms around his neck.

Maybe, just maybe, prayer works.

Twenty-Five

I swear I'm living in Hollywood tonight. I do my best to step where Adrian steps, to keep my body angled just as his is, as he leads me through winding tunnels and hallways hidden inside his house. Who the fuck has something like this?

People that are like me do. Paranormals that are high-ranking. Ones that have to stay alive to protect our species.

It seems like hours before the cool breeze sweeps across my flushed cheeks, having just climbed out of a hidden window that sits just above the grass. It blends perfectly with the exterior of the house. Camouflaged so there's no proof it's a window from outdoors. From the inside, the view is the same as any other pane of glass. I may be nerding out just a bit about it.

Adrian takes my hand, leading me from his backyard to one of his neighbors through a bundle of bushes that are definitely just for aesthetics. The damn thorns hurt like a bitch, cutting into my thighs, hands, and jacket. Just another set of clothing ruined today. We slink from shadow to shadow, keeping ourselves hidden until he clicks the keyless fob for an unassuming silver Honda, tucked into an alley several blocks away.

Before he can drive off, I throw my arms around him again. Pulling him into me. He holds me back this time, inhaling deeply. A calmness finally starts to settle, knowing he's safe, for now. But this isn't over. It's just the beginning.

Salvatore sent beasts after my man tonight, intending to kill him, all because I refused to. Sal will keep sending his band of murderers after him. He won't stop until Adrian's heart does.

Unless... A dark seed takes root.

"I'm going to kill Salvatore Danarius."

Adrian lets me go, tucking a wave behind my ear.

"We're going to talk later. We need to go."

Reaching across me, he pulls the seat belt into place, the satisfying *click* his cue to fasten his own. As if there wasn't an assassination attempt on him tonight, he leisurely takes us from the city.

We're well into the suburbs when he finally stops at a Target. He remains mute as we shuffle through the store, tossing food, clothing, toiletries, and a few books in the cart he pushes. No one would suspect a thing. Humans likely only think movie characters go into hiding. Not the average suburban-looking couple idling next to them at checkout.

Nearly five hundred dollars later, Adrian loads everything into the trunk before driving away again. It's another hour before he pulls into another suburban neighborhood. These houses are reminders of historic colonial homes tucked away and forgotten. They've been well maintained, but it's obvious they've aged with time.

The car pulls into the drive of a white-sided home, the worst looking one on the long street of packed houses. The garage door rises and then closes snugly behind us, leaving us in pitch-black darkness.

We're quiet as we move the bags from the trunk. My temper threatening to bubble over. The urge to slam him into the wall and demand answers, all-consuming. But, I remain calm, for both our sakes. Adrian is not the one I'm furious with.

The inside of the house is nothing like the outside. Decorated a bit more like a bachelor pad with leather couches and an outdated coffee table. Curtains that clearly weren't purchased to match the house, but block out the outside world. It's simple but clean. Clearly looked after, but not lived in.

"Are you going to tell me what's going on?" The question tumbles from my lips before I can stop it. My impatience wearing thin at once again being kept at arm's length.

He's frozen, bent at the waist, arm extended, ready to place the orange juice into the door of the fridge. Moments pass where he stays in that very position before he finally gingerly places the juice in its spot, slowly closing the door. Hands braced against the edges of the unit, his back muscles roll beneath his shirt. Fingers curled around the metal, his breathing deep as if trying to control himself.

When he spins to face me, his eyes are glowing brighter than I've ever seen. The luminescence makes me take a step back as he stalks toward me. *Step. Step. Click. Click. Step.* Until my back collides with the counter.

"Ari," he groans.

I thought it was vampires that moved with grace and speed. Apparently so does Adrian Alexander. He's hoisted me onto the counter, his narrow hips positioned between my spread legs, lips pressed firmly against my own. For the first time, I do nothing to fight my pull toward him. Whether it's the pairing or just my attraction to him growing is unclear. Still, it's the question that weasels its way into my thoughts nearly every second of every day.

My insides heat. A temperature so scorching, I crack an eye to be sure I didn't catch fire. Hands in my hair and braced on my cheek, he devours me. I'm arched into him, hand fisted in his shirt between us, desperate for more. Damn near dying to have every inch of him pressed against me. Just as I shift forward, wrapping my legs around him, I feel him there. Between my thighs. Poised. Ready. Rock solid. I want him to take me. Right here on this old granite countertop.

The streak of his tongue across the seam of my mouth distracts me from his hand traveling beneath my top, lithe fingers yanking down the cups of my bra to expose me to his touch.

A moan escapes as he bites my taut nipple through my t-shirt, nudging me toward his eager mouth.

"Adrian," his name a breathy moan. A plea.

His lips curve across my neck just after letting go of my nipple. "Don't." *Nip.* "Say." *Squeeze.* "My." *Kiss.* "Name." *Pull.* "Like." Another brush of lips before nipping my flesh, eliciting a whimper. "That."

A warning. One I am too frantic and horny to abide by. Fighting against his hold on my hair and teeth at my collarbone, I work his shirt free of him. It's not the first time I've seen Adrian without one. There's a lot of working out that goes on at the safe houses, but to feel him up close is an entirely unique version of sensory overload. To run my fingertips over the taut flesh of his abdomen. The muscles rippling and flexing under my touch.

"Fuck." *Kiss.* "Me."

"No." As if cold water had been splashed on us, he steps away. The connection instantly gone, while the moisture in my panties still lingers behind.

I should be upset about being rejected when he so clearly wanted me only moments ago. But I'm pissed. A raging fire building within.

Deep Breath.

Breathe, Ari.

Breathe, goddammit.

Prying my eyes open once more, my mouth presses into a straight line. He leans against the fridge, his frown deepening as if I'm the one who rejected him. *That's rich.*

"What the hell is wrong with you? You won't talk to me. You kidnap me to wherever this is. Get me all hot and bothered and then won't even man up and screw me."

With a heavy sigh, he runs his hands through his hair before meeting my stare again. His eyes are still glowing. Casting a spray of light across his thick lashes. The piercing vibrancy making me shift in my spot on the counter.

He's slow to come toward me again. Slipping his shirt back into place as he does. Hands gripping each thigh, he spreads my legs once more shifting to stand between them. I do my best to resist his pull, but he's stronger. *Dammit.*

"Ari. Baby." Bright eyes meet mine. "I will give you anything in this world but that. Not until I know you... want... it."

He is completely daft. Of course, I wanted sex with a hot guy. My eye twitches, knowing how out of control my libido is right now. All the stress of the past few months compiling every day.

"Fine." I push him away, hopping from the counter. "At least tell me what the hell happened tonight."

He recounts his evening, never turning to face me as he does. He'd been prepared knowing an attack was coming. He knew what it would mean for me to refuse killing him. That knowledge of him being my Pair the secret everyone kept from me for who knows how long.

Even if I chose not to accept him and the bond. Even if I hated him. A small sliver of me would die with him. For the rest of my life, that loss would fester like an infection. It's what my mom described as a bond similar to the mates werewolves and vampires experience.

Sal sent the whole gambit after him tonight. Two wolf-shifters, a hitman, a Witch so dark, even the veins lining her body appear black, and a phoenix — one Adrian thought died hundreds of years ago.

"Wait, how old are you?"

He gives me a wry look, shifting the steaks around in the pan. The sizzle is as intoxicating as the scent. I'm nearly salivating, ready to ingest the filet mignons we purchased and the garlic mashed potatoes. I honestly have no idea how I'm not on my *600-lb Life* with the way I can consume calories.

"Two hundred and seventy-four."

With a giggle, I gain his attention again. His eyebrow cocking at the girlish sound. "Ew, I'm supposed to marry an old man. Gross."

He lunges forward then. Peppering my face in kisses as I squeal to get away from him. Really, I don't want to, though. These are those moments you read about in romantic comedies, the ones you hope for someday. It almost makes me believe I might be happy with him in the distant future. That there's more to his icy demeanor than he lets on. I want to get to know him.

That's new.

Just as quickly as he reached for me, he refocuses on cooking. His story of tonight continues. It's almost too much listening to this detailed recap of the night. Slipping between the walls, to keep watch of what was happening to his home. His possessions. The sound of Salvatore's snarl through speakerphone when they didn't find him there.

Our meal passes with comfortable conversation, our choice topics having nothing to do with the situations we've found ourselves in. I'm surprised by how easy it is with him. Just the two of us tucked away in this little house.

As we prepare for bed, he shows me to a guest room, three doors down from his. It's decorated much the same as the rest of the house. So different from his home. There are no pictures or paintings of any sort on the walls. The shelves and dresser are sprinkled with knickknacks reminiscent of his life. Accumulating here over the years.

Just as quickly as we arrived in the room, he leaves for his own. The both of us in need of a shower and a few minutes alone to compose ourselves. Or maybe just me. My body still roars with life. Electricity shooting through it remembering the feel of his hands on my breasts hours ago. His taste still on my tongue despite the delicious dinner he prepared.

I need to get a grip.

I climb into bed with one of the books we got at Target. I don't read as much as I used to, but it seemed like a smart idea to help me pass the time. Yet I never make it past the first paragraph of page one. My eyes won't focus. My mind replaying the vision of me walking through his home tonight. My heart hammering convinced he's not safe even though he's just down the hall.

With a sigh I turn out the light and nuzzle down under the comforter.

An old house like this is bound to creak at night. Its bones straining against the raging elements outside. Determined to make the simplest sounds come across eerie and ominous. It's not long before the anxiety of sleeping alone, in an unfamiliar space, forces me from my bed.

The door groans as I tiptoe into Adrian's room. I planned to sneak in and just slip under the comforter without him knowing, but his voice startles me as I lift the edge.

"What are you doing here?"

On a swallow, I answer, "With everything going on, I just..." My voice trails off, not wanting to admit I was terrified tonight. Scared of losing him. Petrified to let him out of my sight. The spike of adrenaline at every shadow or noise, fear that Sal has found him and his luck won't hold next time.

Without needing to hear the rest, he lifts the blue duvet, cocking his head to signal me to climb in. I do. Lying flat on my back. Stiff as a board. He curls into me, his head on my shoulder, arm wrapped around my waist.

"Sleep. I've got you."

My heart flutters. Just a little.

Twenty-Six

Brushing grazes trace the feathers inked across my back, pulling me from the most glorious sleep I've had in quite some time. With a heavy sigh, last night comes back into sharp focus: The pile of rubble that now makes up Adrian's home. Crippling fear nearly stopped me in my tracks at the thought of losing him. A loss I can't handle. Our escape to yet another safe house hidden in plain sight. His silent welcome into bed beside him — whether he knew my reasons for coming to it or not. It was too much to bear alone.

I knew the moment we arrived, this house was different. A space personal for Adrian. A private sanctuary.

"It's gorgeous," he breathes behind me. Warmth brushes against my tangled hair and bare shoulder. A shudder running through my body at his inspection.

My muscles tense and shift as he continues to explore the exposed skin. The tank top I'm wearing is by no means risque. It's cut revealing enough of my back and the entirety of the rear side of my arms for him to ogle. Tuck once asked me about the crimson, tiger, and marigold feathers that line the back of my arms. My own representation of my wings. I'd told him the truth. How having the array of feathers etched onto my skin made me feel just a bit less alone in this world.

"Are you going to tell me about it?" Firm lips press against my exposed shoulder, making me wiggle, keeping my head turned away from him.

Problem one: my morning dragon breath. The primary reason, to keep him from catching the tears pooling behind my eyes at his fingering and questioning. That small piece of me that was my curated "family" since I turned eighteen and had it done.

"No."

He shifts behind me, his bare chest pressing against my back. "I want to see the whole thing."

With a shrug, I shuffle to my knees, pulling the tank over my head, balling it into my fist. I don't bother to cover myself, before lying face down, head rotated in the opposite direction. I know the moment he spots the single cobalt and gold feather in the center of my back, nestled below where the neck of my bird's feathers branch out in a brilliant spread of burnt orange and marigolds. He sucks in a breath, stealing all the oxygen in the room for himself.

There's no denying the feather is a near-perfect match to the one of his I found in his damp grass months ago. What I won't tell him is he's the exact phoenix I imagined as a child. The one I would find someday and have little Firebird babies of our own with. The answer to my loneliness. After meeting him and seeing his bird up close, it made me wonder if I'd ever met him — even for the briefest of moments as an infant — before I was torn away from my parents.

Even if I had, newborn me wouldn't have a memory of him. It's more likely the Pairing between us brought images of him to my dreams. A way to tell me I wasn't alone. The surety that my soul matched that of another Phoenix.

Throughout my adolescence and even into adulthood, I dreamt of him. Now he's real. He's here, stroking intentional fingers down my spine tracing the perimeter of the feather that belongs to him.

"Don't ask," I groan, shoving my face into the pillow.

"It's mine." His voice is soft. Quiet. Gentler than I've ever heard. It's enough to make me turn to look at him. His gaze still trained on that single spot. The glow that always seems to happen around me, blinding. Luminescent.

"Adrian, I really don't want to talk about it. Or my tattoo. I want to..."

His eyes snap up to mine. Locking me in place.

I want to be with you.

I want us to be safe. You. Me. My family. All of us.

I want to stay locked in this bubble with you, where you aren't an asshole.

My cowardice keeps me from allowing myself to recite the list out loud. Releasing my tank, I keep my back to him, shifting it back into place. My only guard of protection. From me. Him. Both, maybe.

"I want to find Salvatore. What's our next move?"

There's no point in turning around. I cannot bear to see that icy glare he wears like a coat of armor.

"You think you can just walk up to his front door and shoot him? You're more naïve than you pretend not to be."

"Fuck you, Adrian." The cop in me sits up straight, shooting invisible daggers. The hitwoman roars to life. "I've known Sal a long time —"

"Not longer than I have," he grunts, throwing the comforter aside as if it personally offended him.

"Sorry, I'm not sorry for wanting to protect my family and others like us from being slaughtered." The words a violent hiss as I launch myself from the mattress.

The door handle cracking against the wall should be enough to stop me in my tracks as I stalk away from him. My sure steps taking me back to the room he declared as mine the night before. I need space from... him.

Who does he think he is? How dare he think he can tell me what to do. I'm not naïve. I know how to kill, even if I don't understand this underworld the way he does. It's what Sal groomed me to do for years now. Ruthless assassin. No remorse.

That was true enough, not long ago. Except, now, the guilt has finally found me. My family falling back into my life, changing things. The meaning of Adrian's massive hand around my throat altering my internal compass.

"Have you calmed down now?"

Of course, he followed me. His arms cross his bare chest, shoulder resting against the doorframe, that smug smirk pulling at those firm lips. His legs crossed at the ankle, revealing just how nonplussed he was by my tantrum.

"Adrian," I breathe, running my fingers through my hair. "I can't do this with you."

I hadn't planned on doing this now. Yes, it's the reason I sought him out last night, but all at once my chest is tight. I'm suddenly unsure. But if I don't say everything I'm keeping deadbolted inside, I won't be able to do what I need to do with Sal.

He takes two steps toward me. I take three in retreat. My hands rise in front of me as if they will keep him at a distance. But, nothing keeps Adrian Alexander from getting what he wants.

"I can't do this with you," I repeat. "I can't be with you. I can't do this bickering married couple thing we do. I know we're paired and I'm not saying no to that, but I can't be worried about you and do what I need to do. I can't have you on my mind constantly distracting me. I don't know how to commit myself to someone else, but somehow, without my permission, my heart and body have decided for me. My mind though..." I release a breath, as he moves close enough that only a sliver of air can pass between our torsos, lifting my chin to meet his gaze. "My mind is still in control."

The words tumbled free before I settled on what the sentences would be. My unfiltered feelings released into the universe. Stepping out of his hold, I round up clean clothing from the small loveseat.

"Is this because I wouldn't have sex with you?"

His words stop me mid-step. I'd nearly forgotten he rejected me last night. The hurt and embarrassment wash over me anew. Shallow breaths filter past my lips as I pivot to face him.

"No. Contrary to what you might believe, I can live without your dick. This is about protecting the people I love and care about. Sorry, you made the list." More of that honesty, I should have kept locked away.

With a shrug, I make a second attempt to retreat into the adjoining bathroom. His movements stopping mine in the same breath, turning me to face him. A firm grip on the back of my neck. A squeeze. His hold enough to force my face up to his as he captures my mouth in a possessive kiss.

He was supposed to walk away. He was supposed to understand, but instead, he's here, with his body pressed to mine as he ignites my internal flames.

It's only seconds before the clothing gripped in my hands is forgotten, my fingers releasing them to hold on to his warm sides instead.

Milliseconds more before we fall to a heap on the mattress. The bedding the exact way I left it the night before. Barely ruffled.

His lips and hands explore my body. Devouring me, learning my curves as I pant beneath him. The word *hypocrite* ricochets through my head. Only moments ago, I'd told him sex wasn't something I needed from him. Yet, here we are, rolling in a frenzied heap, with our clothes as the only barrier between our heated skin.

His hardened length presses between my legs, the sleep shorts doing nothing to guard me against the nudge of his head. There's no stopping the roll of my hips forward. A need to get impossibly closer. To feel him inside me.

I can't. I won't cave. I just said I wouldn't.

"Adrian."

He hums against the pulse of my neck.

"Adrian." My tone more urgent this time.

He finally pulls back to look at me. "I told you I won't give you that, but there are plenty of other things I can give you."

A wicked gleam morphs his emerald irises into dancing embers of green and gold.

Fingers looped into the waistband of my shorts, he slides them down my thighs, pulling my panties along with them. There are many women who do the whole commando thing, but it always makes me cringe. The sole reason I couldn't do ballet as a kid. They expected no undies under the tights and leotards.

No. Thank you!

The small memory quickly fades as the extended inhale from him at the apex of my thighs pulls me back to the present. *Well, that's a first.* He does it again, before running a finger down my slick folds. The same precision and ease he trailed the feathers on my back this morning carried into this moment.

My body writhes against his touch, minimal as it is. I want to be closer to him. I want more. As if he can read my mind, firm lips pull at my bud, suckling it like a sweet fruit, before dragging his teeth, making my nerves shoot electric bolts into my lower belly.

"Fuck!" I bark, my fingers sinking into his silky hair.

He only chuckles against my soaked flesh, fingers pressing harder into the meat of my thighs, spreading me impossibly wider. His warm breath fans over me and all I want is to stay lost in this moment. To feel Adrian consume every part of me.

His exploration continues, slow and torturous. There's no rush as he licks, sucks, and tastes all of me, the torrent of an orgasm building within me.

"Adrian." His name a huffing breath, as my fingers yank at his hair.

"Do it," he challenges. His breath tickles my sensitive flesh before his tongue pierces me.

Sensations I've never felt soar through me. With each passing second, the need to keep my fire at bay increases. With another expert flick of his tongue, my release coats his mouth. His lips. His face glistening with the evidence of what he does to me. It's not my release dripping down his cheek that catches my eye, though. It's the carefree smile. All his pristine white teeth showing, the corners of his eyes crinkling.

Did I just make Adrian Alexander... happy?

Twenty-Seven

It takes two beers, thirty chicken wings, and five episodes of *Criminal Minds* for Adrian to finally fall asleep on the couch. It's my only chance. He'd have a conniption if he knew what I actually had planned. After hours of him pleasuring me every which way — minus actually having sex with me — the plan came to me. My resolve hardened. My determination locked in.

I may have become an incapable *human* these last few months, but I've always handled life on my own. It was me who forged the badass homicide detective I am today. Much of it was me that became the killing machine Sal needed so badly. With Oliver's and my mom's help, I've learned how to truly accept what I am, becoming a stronger version of Ari in the process. No matter who has been there to guide me along the way, I did the work. That was me. It will be me that ends this.

It's Wednesday night. There's only one place Salvatore ever goes on Wednesdays. The underground club located beneath one of the many Chicago skyscrapers. Hidden away from the general public, so only those with an invitation could find it. Normally, I would only walk in at his request. Show Sal I can hang with the big boys, but not tonight.

For this to work, he can't see me coming. He'll know the moment he looks into my eyes, I'm only there for one reason. To end him. To destroy everything he is and what he stands for. This world will be a much better place without him. I will make it so no one ever has to bow to him again or fall to one of the hands he's hired.

It's a silent night as I slink from Adrian's house, a zip hoodie I found in the closet wrapped around me. I keep it bunched high around my chin, inhaling his scent. Hoping like hell it won't be the last time I get to.

I'm not stupid. My plan to walk in and kill Sal on his own turf is risky. The possibility I don't walk back out is high. If he pulls one of his custom guns on me, my Phoenix may not be enough to pull me back from the brink of death, no matter how much I wish, hope, or pray for it. I'm willing to make that sacrifice so no one else will have to.

Those that I've come to love and adore flash unbidden through my mind. Tuck. Talia. Oliver. Gomez. My mom. Every phoenix I've gotten to know these past few months. My dad.

A choked cry escapes me. No matter what we've done, he lies in the same place. Frozen in that stalled state, he put himself in. I hope this won't be my last chance to meet him. I need more time.

Shaking the sadness from my mind, I stalk forward. My peripheral vision serves as my best friend, my only intel to reveal if

I'm being followed. I've made it five blocks up and three over, the location my Uber will meet me. He pulls up only moments after I make it to the curb in front of the address I gave him. The inside of the gray-sided house shrouded in darkness. Not even a porch light to cut the dark, signifying it's occupied. But the manicured lawn and his and hers rocking chairs on the front porch tell me it is. A happy couple living their lives together. Not a care in the world.

A future a part of me wishes I could have too.

The drive into the city stretches, my thoughts whirling through my mind. I try multiple times to talk myself out of what I plan to do. To think of what my death would do to my family and Adrian, but it's them who I am thinking of. It's them I want to have a peaceful future and not fear being hunted by a power-hungry warlock. The same way Mom and Dad worked to create a more stable world for me to come back to, I have to do the same for them.

"Be careful out there," my driver calls as I climb out of the backseat. The warning ominous as if he is aware of the things I plan to do tonight. As if he knows I happily toe the line of danger.

Draped in darkness, I enter my apartment. Tonight the shadows are my only friends as I stare at nothing, letting them circle me. It's hours before I change into attire worthy of entering Prime 79 — one of many exclusive clubs Salvatore owns. His safe zone I'm happy to infiltrate.

The bodycon dress fits me like a glove. Every curve on display for men to gawk at, eye fucking me like the desperate dogs they are. I chose it purposely. There's not much left to the imagination, my back exposed under angled strips of fabric, and the low cut V in the front, giving me the appearance of cleavage I wish I actually had.

For as delectable as I appear, I'm strapped to the nines. Four knives secured to my body in various locations. Sal's gun tucked into the built-in holster on the right and a backup Glock on the left. The pins holding the front of my hair off my forehead in an artistic swoop of waves, really miniature sheathed razors capable of slicing through flesh like any other blade.

Lips coated in a wine lipstick so dark, the color appears nearly black in the shadows.

With a final look in the mirror and a deep breath puffing out my chest, I'm ready.

I take another Uber to the location of the black and chrome skyscraper that hides Prime 79 beneath it. Only those on the exclusive list would even know there's anything two stories below the lobby. The entrance classic, glass double doors where the security scans for facial recognition before allowing entrance to the elevator at the far end, slightly obscured by an abstract marble slab. By day, it elevates you to the penthouse. By night descends to the underground — where debauchery is the way of life.

My heels click loudly across the marble floor as I strut forward, drowning out the loud beating of my heart. The clock is ticking. Dwindling down to the moment Adrian wakes from the spot I left him in. I'd debated leaving a note. Opted against it, knowing he'll eventually figure it out. That there will be no hiding from him once he does. At least this way it buys me time.

I hope he doesn't come for me. I need him to stay safe. That's why I'm doing this.

Adrian, I'm sorry.

My last chance to take a steadying breath is the chime of the elevator. The *whoosh* of the opening doors tosses my ends just enough to break contact with my shoulders. My last chance to back out. To walk away and find a better plan. A safer plan. One that doesn't sacrifice me or potentially innocent people downstairs fucking and drinking without a care in the world.

No. There's no turning back. He has taken enough from us.

Stepping into the elevator, the guard's eyes narrow as I turn to face him before widening. The recognition hit him too late. Who I am. I recognized him immediately. A lower-ranking flunky on Sal's roster, but one that he trusts enough to man this building.

The sixty seconds it takes to descend the two stories seems to stretch on. Sweat beading at the base of my neck, down my back, and between my breasts. It's not fear. It's anticipation.

Sal will be the first kill I've ever actually wanted. Needed.

The heavy bass of the music and flashing neon lights assault me as I step out of the elevator, straight onto the black marble floors of the club. He's spared no expense decorating this place. The plush seating areas and high-top tables, plated in the same ebony marble. Top-shelf liquor only. The servers dressed to the nines, as is expected for all guests.

Nearly every square inch is filled. Bodies moving about, boisterous laughter flitting around me. A man dressed in a custom-fitted suit bumps into me, eyes roving down my body before flashing an apologetic grin. If not for the two women that drag him along a proposition would be the only thought on his mind. He wouldn't be the first. *Bore.*

It's a battle moving through the main floor of the club; the area Sal calls the commons. By normal club standards, these would be your VIPs. The ones that turn up their noses at everyone while they sip their drinks and pretend their shit doesn't stink. Not here, though. At Prime 79, they are the bottom feeders. Scavengers looking to sink their teeth into the first person to get them into the restricted areas. A small chuckle escapes me. How true that statement might be. How many are "other" like me?

Shoving my way through the throng of sweaty bodies, I head for the bowels of the club. Tucked in the coves where the private rooms are located, a narrow stairwell leads to a small loft area where Salvatore's private lounge can be found. His resolve as to who may enter, not shifting much in all the years I've known him. The frosted glass door emerges as if rising from the floor as I clear the top of the spiral staircase leading to the secluded area. Two guards stand outside of it. One addressing me with a smirk and a nod. Brian — I think — has always been partial to me. Gifting me unwanted winks and not-so-subtle ass grabs.

Without question, he opens the door for me. In unison, both guards slip to the side, allowing me entrance. The space is no larger than my living room, with suede curved couches of onyx lining one wall complemented by low-back armchairs. Several women lay sprawled across the couch beside Sal, one with her lips suctioned to the side of his neck. Two other men are in the room. Their lips cresting their tumblers of liquor.

It takes longer than I expected for Sal to notice my presence. His eyes finally peel open as the second woman removes her hand from his crotch, where she'd been rubbing him as if her life depended on it. It's disgusting. Sal has been married for God knows how long, but here he is, letting random women feel him up. It's not like I haven't seen it before, but my time shifting away from being his pawn has taken me from admiring him to realizing what a waste of space he really is.

"Ah, Ari. Join us." He gestures, arms wide, drink sloshing over the rim of the glass.

Cocking a perfectly manicured brow, I'm ready to perform. This night entirely dependent on him believing I'm here for nothing more than a bit of dirty fun.

"Of course." Brian appears behind me, as silent as a cat, passing me a tumbler of what I assume is bourbon. Raising my glass, I take my first sip. The tiniest one I can muster. I need my head clear. I'll only get one chance.

Sal's eyes stay locked on me as he shoos the woman away, draping one arm across the back of the sofa, bringing what's left of his drink to his lips.

"To what do I owe the pleasure?" It's not an actual question. But a confrontation. The number of times I'd declined to come here, the suspicion of my unannounced appearance is clear in the pinch of his brow and minuscule purse of his lips.

"Am I not to join you for fun? Does one missed kill really exclude me from enjoying…" I allow my words to drift off as I purposely eye the men to my immediate right. They are attractive enough. Men I would have slept with in a heartbeat. That was before. Before… Adrian.

"Well, take a seat." He pats the spot next to him. "Or do you need to stand for what you actually came to do?"

My gaze darts back to him. The tiniest tell that he's thrown me off balance. *It's now or never.* With a turn of the glass in my right hand, I pull the gun he gifted me with my left, pointing it directly at where his heart should be.

Twenty-Eight

ADRIAN

I wake to a silent house, alone on the couch, with a blanket anchored around me. Ari had definitely been beside me. Checking the time, I think nothing of it. It's after midnight. No doubt she likely went to bed. Preferably mine. As much as she drives me up a fucking wall, I loved sleeping next to her last night.

I wasn't looking for a relationship when she came barging into my life. From the very first night she set out to follow me, thinking she was some sort of super spy, I felt the bond. Anyone could have spotted her. Should have. Most aren't trained the way I am, though. Programmed to watch their surroundings with a relentless focus. As Second I don't get the luxury of a fuckup. Everyone depends on me all the time.

I'd have it no other way. It's supposed to be an honor to be of my bloodline. Yet, I'll never be proud of the blood that runs through my veins. Phoenixes in my line are exceedingly rare these days. It's better that way. A smaller pool of enemies.

I'm wandering through the lower level of the house. Every light is out. No sign of Ari. *Upstairs, then.* I check her bedroom first. After fooling around for hours, the bed remains disheveled. The memories assault me. The scent of her arousal still thick in the air. I wanted to sleep with her. Every time she looks at me with those big blue eyes, the desire to drop to my knees and give myself to her is overwhelming.

She'd asked me to fuck her. Repeatedly. I kept my composure, knowing what it would mean if we did. The irreversible position we would be in. The fear that she'll reject me still cripples me some days, so I refuse to seal our bond. Not yet.

Her room was untouched. So is mine. Panic creeps into my chest and then my throat. My hoarse voice calling out for her.

Silence.

No answer.

"Ari," I bark, sounding pissed but really just terrified they took her and my dumbass had been asleep instead of protecting her.

Surely I would have heard something. If someone was here, if they'd taken her, I'd know.

Racing back downstairs, I'm frantic as I search beneath the pillows on the couch for my phone. If she left, there's only one person who might know where.

"Where is she?" I growl.

Tuck's silent on the other end. He's used to my temper. The asshole everyone gets to interact with, an accurate representation of who I've become. It's not just reserved for her, even though I'm sure she believes that. Ari just gets an extra dose, because no one can push my buttons the way she does.

"I don't know…" Those three words riddled with anxiety. He knows something is wrong too. "She's supposed to be there with you. Where the hell did she go?"

Shame drains my energy. "I don't know."

"Get back here. Now."

Not even bothering with shoes, I race out to the garage. The door barely opens before I'm peeling out and down the road. I'm well out of sight of my house when it occurs to me, I may not have even closed the door. I don't care.

I have to find her. Before someone else does.

Salvatore already knows of our connection. Our Pairing. I have no doubt in my mind he's not above using her to get to me. My unique set of gifts, a prize that would make him nearly invincible if he could siphon them. That much we learned. That's why he wants what flows through my veins. Dead or alive, it doesn't matter. He wants the power I possess.

There are more cars on the road than should be. Their sole purpose: to piss me off. The traffic always funneling into the small pockets of open space I'm darting in and out of. Like me, Tuck lives in a single-family home on the outskirts of the city. Our need for space more important than convenience.

He's outside waiting for me, clearly tracking my location to know when I would arrive.

"How do we find her?"

He waves me inside, down to the basement, where we keep certain prisoners sometimes. The cement walls of their cells laced with the metal alloy that stifles our magical gifts and shifting abilities.

A few weeks back, we captured one of Salvatore's inner circle. One of the grunts that spent enough time around his operations to give us some answers we needed. It was around that time Tuck stopped bringing Ari here. He didn't want her to know what kind of man he really is. His dark side kept far from her inquisitive nature.

Tucker is one of the nicest guys I know, with a deadly violent streak. We all have our roles to play. When it comes to torture and information, he's our man. A practice his mother often doesn't approve of. He transforms from the caring boy next door to the Joker incarnate, giving no mercy to those that move against paranormal law. He shows no leniency to humans versus our kind. They all get the same treatment.

"Hello, Jared."

A thickset guy, at least four inches taller than me, tied to a basic metal chair, looks up. His head moves so slowly you'd think it weighed an actual ton. His lip busted so wide it appears more like pulverized flesh than a single curve as the bottom of his mouth. One eye is swollen shut, the bruising leaving purple in the dust, and settling on a slate black.

Where he always smirked or laughed at us when he first arrived, now he looks at us with hesitation. The lowering of his brows a telltale sign of his fear of what we might do next. How much more pain we'll inflict. He knows he won't leave here alive. He can't. It's not an option.

"Where would Salvatore be tonight?"

Jared bows his head again like there's no way he can hold it up any longer.

Striding to the corner, Tuck grabs a bat — made of that same metal alloy — matching the chair we strapped this piece of shit to. Angling the bat under Jared's chin, he forces his gaze back to us.

"Now Jared, we've become such good friends. I think you're going to want to answer me," he hums. The tone menacing. Terrifying. I always thought I was a bad fucker until I realized how deranged Tuck's other half is.

"Prime." He coughs. Blood specks coat his dirty jeans and the floor at his feet. A small puddle of dark liquid splashes to the floor as he coughs again. "Prime." A heaving breath. "79."

Tuck drops the bat from beneath his chin only a second after I've already started sprinting for the door, stopping only long enough to slip on a pair of Tuck's sneakers by the main entrance.

Hearing that name out of his mouth, I know Salvatore didn't take Ari. She went to him. Just like the beaten-down warlock in the basement, Ari also knows Salvatore's movements. His intricacies. His way of life. She left to go after him. She said she'd kill him, and I brushed it off, knowing she was shaken and scared.

It was a problem I thought we'd have time to solve. My girl does things differently. That brilliant firecracker takes matters into her own hands. I've seen it in the way she talks about him now; the puppet no longer willing to be controlled by her puppeteer.

She was strong. Invincible. Unstoppable when she found us, but reuniting with her kind and her family has only heightened that. Maturing her in a way I can't put into actual words.

The Honda swerves through the downtown streets, careening through yellow lights trying to get to her. I need to get to her. My chest tightens, resignation settling in my gut — I may not make it in time. Anything could happen before I get there.

I refuse to waste time finding a legitimate parking spot as I pull up outside the imposing glass structure of a building. It's ominous in the daylight but at night a tower of nightmares. Two guards stop me at the doors to the lobby.

"Sir, you can't enter." One holds out an arm, keeping me from crossing the threshold. Fuck him. I'm walking in there.

"You'll let me in." A grin pulling at the corner of my mouth.

"No, Sir. I won't."

"You will. Tell Salvatore Adrian Alexander is here to see him."

Both sets of eyes go wide, the smaller one taking a few steps to the side to speak into a sleek watch on his wrist. He throws us a nod, both men leading me to an elevator I hadn't even noticed.

The doors slip open immediately, the initial guard pushing a few buttons before stepping back out, eyes focused on me as the doors close. Just as a guard left me in the elevator, another retrieves me as the doors shift open, gripping me lightly behind the arm and guiding me forward.

He doesn't talk to me at all, allowing me to take in the surrounding club. I've heard about this place. Anyone in our world has. It's just as it's been described. Dancing strobe lights, nearly naked women, and hungry men. Endless cocktails and liquor on every surface. The dark blue hue casting the place in shifting shadows.

I'm led up a flight of stairs. That thick hand holding me in place at a door of frosted glass. Clearly, it's meant to lead me to a private room. One I'm sure Ari and Salvatore are in.

She has to be here. Please let her be here.

The door swings open. Salvatore seated on the couch, ankle crossed over his knee, wearing a smug grin. Ari with her gun pointed at his chest. There are others in the room. Their positions at the far reaches of the space, inconsequential. Unimportant.

She's here. The tightness in my chest relaxes just a little. *She's here.*

"Ari," I breathe.

It's as if the sound of her name broke whatever trance she was in. Her eyes flicker back in my direction — an almost imperceptible motion. The second enough for Sal to slip the gun from his lower back. The distraction enough for her to lose the focus she needed to take her shot.

The entire scene plays out in slow motion, my legs heavy as if filled with hardened cement as I try to run for her the instant the gunshot rings out. Her chest curved into a C, hair flying forward as she falls, bright blood glistening around the bullet hole just over the edge of the fabric covering her breasts.

I catch her just before she smacks into the marble flooring beneath us. She doesn't move. Limp as she sags into my arms.

Turn the page for bonus chapters from Adrian

Bonus Chapter 1

ADRIAN

There's a woman following me. I feel her presence vibrating through my body the same as my phone in my pocket. Keeping an eye on her, I yank it free.

"What do you need?" I grunt.

"Hello, to you too," Tuck's voice comes through the other line. He's the only one never bothered by my broody demeanor. He either jokes it away or travels to that dark, twisted place where he sometimes exists to brood with me.

"What do you need?" I repeat.

She smoothly passes between two people ahead of her. She's just close enough that a gust of wind may send her scent to me. A deep inhale of the air gives me nothing.

Not quite close enough.

From here, I can't tell if she's human or paranormal. Only that her eyes are like blue sapphires glinting in the light. A perfect compliment to the rays of sunshine reflecting off the skyscrapers as dusk settles. Those eyes. I feel like I know them.

"Adrian! Adrian!" Tuck barks my name. He'd clearly been talking to me, but I was focused on her. The closer she gets, the more my insides seem drawn to her. It's an odd tugging sensation within. One I've never felt. A rub at my sternum doing nothing to cast it away.

"Sorry, I was distracted," my voice trails off, my eyes following her every move.

My gaze rakes down her frame. Long legs. Fit, but not thin. Gorgeous brown waves that move every time she does. Oddly enough, from here, she kind of reminds me of Tuck. That thought is enough to refocus my attention.

"By who?" His tone so incredulous, my head snaps toward the speaker.

The muscles of my jaw flex as I pull my gaze from her. "There's a woman following me."

He huffs a laugh. "The good kind of following or the type that requires a different side of me?"

"Chill, Tucker. I don't know," I answer honestly.

There's shuffling in the background as if his sheets are brushing across his bare skin. It wouldn't be the first time he's called me from bed after fucking his girlfriend. Excuse me... making love.

He chuckles. "Have you seen her before?"

"No. But I —" My voice stalls, unsure how to put it into words. There's no easy way to describe how I knew she was there. My body can sense her in a way that shouldn't be possible. Only two options are feasible: blood relative or...

No. Absolutely not.

I refuse to let my mind go there.

"Okay, so... are you going to talk to her?"

"Funny, Tuck. I don't think she's following me so that I can ask her out for a beer."

He snorts several times, my nose scrunching in response. That Tuck finds humor in his parent's second being followed is ridiculous.

"Seriously Adrian. I've never seen you with anyone. When was the last time you even slept with someone?"

A loud groan leaves me. I hate this conversation. The other guys try to bring up the same tired questions with me, and I immediately shut it down. My love life is not up for discussion. I have duties and a ruthless family still out there somewhere. Not all of us strive to find a partner to come home to. Tuck did. Others have, but I'm not them.

"We don't all want to be like you and Talia," I grunt. "Especially since this bubbly life you two have planned together ends the moment one of you meets your Pair."

"Not true." The incredulous tone returns. His sniffle that follows a dead-giveaway he's uncomfortable with the truth I just threw in his face like a weapon. As much as I hate having the relationship discussion from the perspective of finding someone, Tuck hates having it knowing his girlfriend, he's head over heels in love with, isn't his Pair. There is no force in this world or the next that can coerce a Pair bond into existence.

My focus is suddenly torn away from our conversation. I've lost track of her. Spinning in multiple directions, I can't see her anywhere, but I still... feel her. Her presence rings through my insides. Toying with me. Riling me up. Setting me so far on edge, my breathing quickens.

"Adrian, what's wrong with you?" Tuck's voice brings me back.

"I lost her."

"Well, maybe you should have taken my advice."

"Tuck." A warning. Should he continue pushing, I just might snap.

The soles of my dress shoes clap against the steps leading up to the train platform. Maybe she wandered elsewhere. But I know that's not true. My body still dancing with excitement knowing she's near. Regardless, I need to get home. I have things to do.

"Fine. I actually called you because we were able to link those recent deaths back to Danarius."

"Why am I not surprised?"

"Us either. He's killing off big names, Adrian. We know he's got his team of hitmen." He pauses, swallowing loudly. "But from what we've heard, these were all carried out by a woman."

"You're shitting me."

"Wish I was, brother."

"Find out who she is. Bring her to me when you do."

Tuck answers with a grunt. "My way or your way?" I can almost see that sinister grin spread across his innocent face. The dark side Tuck keeps hidden, hoping I agree to his way.

"Mine."

"Understood," he replies. His tone immediately jumps back to the soft-spoken man most of us know. The calm, gentle soul who loves his parents and girlfriend and would do anything for our kind.

"I'm headed home. Call if you find something."

"Will do," he chimes before the line goes dead.

I stuff my phone back in my pocket, continuing to search the train platform. Hands in my pockets, I watch for her through my periphery.

The tugging inside me intensifies, but I can't find her.

Just as the train pulls forward, I gaze to my right. Her long frame, in those skin-tight jeans, coming into view for the briefest of moments before she boards the train. Not once does she look my way. Not to mention she's several cars down.

I could try to convince myself this is nothing more than a coincidence, but my training refuses to allow it. It's a lie I would never wholeheartedly believe anyhow.

There's no relaxing on the train ride home, as I pretend to analyze spreadsheets of budgets. Instead, I study the statistics of the many paranormal murders that continue to happen around this city. The exponential increase has Syriah on edge, especially after she and James were attacked.

Someone came for my family.

Our city.

My city.

This city a place I made home over a hundred years ago. A place with people I care about. A sanctuary with a pecking order that makes sense and provides us all with the checks we need. My family never respected the structure of power. They thrive on a type of cruelty I refuse to be part of. Yet, I know one day they will come for me. I am the son they couldn't bend to their will.

Memories of my childhood swarm me as the train plows forward.

I'm so distracted I don't see the woman creeping closer to me. Where she'd been four cars away before, she's now in the one connected to mine. Her torso straight as she sits about midway through the car, her back to me.

It's only another five minutes before I exit the train. The stop chosen meant to throw her off my trail. I'm not surprised when she follows. Her distance is safe. One that a regular Joe Schmo would never notice because they weren't trained to.

The further I walk, the more my mouth presses into a thin line. The sensations rolling through me are so fucking distracting. Enticing. Damn near seductive.

When I disappear into a restaurant, her steps suddenly still. She only stares momentarily before tucking her hands into her pockets and striding down the street.

I can still sense her. Feel her churning inside me. A sudden desire to possess her drawing me a step back toward the door, but I fight it.

It doesn't take long to catch her. Long strides carrying her back toward the train. She doesn't seem to notice the tides have turned. My body taut with tension as she wanders through the darkening city alone. There is an air of toughness about her. Even so, a woman still shouldn't be walking the streets alone. Not at night. Not in downtown Chicago.

I shouldn't care if she's out here unaccompanied. She's not my responsibility. She's a threat. I can smell it in the scent of her left behind with her trail.

A blanket of darkness has fallen over us before she saunters into a hole-in-the-wall pub. From the outside, it looks like the type of place only college kids can afford to drink in. One that's sure to have sticky floors and toilets that don't flush after nine p.m. The only beer they'll have is cheap and American on tap and forget about top-shelf liquor. It's not in the budget.

Rolling out my neck, I step into the bar. The inside has been kept more than the exterior. A well-maintained and polished bar that stretches nearly the length of the place. Dark wood floors and furniture from this decade. Several patrons line the bar and spot the square tables spread throughout the space. Despite the pop-rock music playing and conversations around the room, the place isn't overly loud. A small mercy if I'm going to sit here and listen to her.

I spot her sitting at the end of the bar. Several men crowd around her, laughing loudly. She quirks a grin as she tosses back a tumbler of dark liquor. She doesn't even wince as she swallows the liquid down. Her throat working as she smirks, making my dick twitch in my pants.

"Couldn't stay away," one guy laughs, draping his arm around her shoulders.

Fury rolls through me. The intensity forcing me to drop into the chair of the table closest to me. It makes no sense. There's no reason for me to respond so strongly to her being with another man. Unless...

No. Fuck right off with that thought, Adrian.

Taking a deep breath, I return my focus to her. She eyes the guy oddly, but the grin remains. "Booth, you better take that arm back before I shoot it off." She winks at him, a second glass placed in her hand without her looking toward the bartender.

The other guys laugh as he removes his arm, hands high in a placating gesture. She only tips her head in acknowledgement. As if to say *touch me again and you die.*

"Luxe, you're supposed to be solving murders, not causing them."

She only shrugs, gulping her drink. "Never said I was going to kill you."

She's a cop. Why the hell is a cop following me?

I sit there watching her for hours. She and her fellow officers shooting the shit. I know her name is Ari now, although they call her Luxe. That same guy, Booth, keeps finding ways to touch her and I want nothing more than to rip his hand from his body. He shouldn't be touching what doesn't belong to him.

"Luxe, we'll see you in the morning."

She waves to her colleagues as they all exit the bar. Not a single one of them noticed me slumped at the table I'd moved to near the corner. I removed my suit jacket and rolled up my sleeves. Mussed up my hair and sat low, hoping her gaze wouldn't drift my way. So far, it seems she hasn't.

I listen to her make idle conversation with the bartender as he continues to slide her drink after drink. Yet, no matter how many she downs, she never seems to cross the line to drunk.

It's only a matter of minutes before a large man sits next to her. His beer half gone, as he slips her a crooked grin.

"I was hoping you would be here tonight," he says, chugging the last of his beer.

She only rakes her gaze over him, downing the contents of her glass before abruptly standing. "Let's go." She cocks her head to the side, signaling for him to follow. And just like a puppy, he does. Wide-eyed with a shit-eating grin on his face.

This time, when a man drapes his arm around her shoulder, she says nothing. I watch the two of them go. That sensation hitting me again. My insides rioting. My Phoenix fighting to chase after her.

It's as if an obvious answer slaps me in the face. One I refuse to believe is true.

She's not...

Bonus Chapter 2
Adrian

Her laughter hits me. The beautiful chorus of it making my insides spark alive. I cannot fucking escape the woman and no matter how rude I am to her, it does nothing to turn off my pull toward her. It won't shut down the feelings that come with what she is to me. Who she'll always be.

Even if she weren't my Pair, I would be attracted to her. She has a tough streak in her. One that makes my dick unnecessarily hard. But she also has a big heart. She wants to do the right thing. Wants to be on the right side.

It doesn't change that she's the hitwoman we've been looking for, but if I'm right, her allegiances have changed. I was her designated target and have been alone with her more times than I'd like to count, but she's not so much as given me the slightest inkling she still intends to kill me.

She said she won't. I wish I could say it took her repeating it more than once to believe her, but it didn't. Yet, I've hung the possibility over her head every chance I get. It's easier to be an ass to her. Easier to keep her at arm's length, so the possessiveness in me doesn't make me do something stupid. Something I'll regret. Something to give her a genuine reason to hate me.

But walking into this room now, listening to her laugh with another man, sends me into a brutal rage. *It's the Pairing*. We become so territorial it can be dangerous even for the people we know won't harm our Pair. Every moment of watching her with other men, whether it be Oliver or Bronson or even her colleagues, the tether holding my control in place withers. Fraying cords set to snap apart at any moment.

So entering the gym to find Oliver sidled in close behind her, takes everything in me to keep my feet rooted in place. She has the squat bar on her shoulders as if she's ready to take the plunge. His body poised at her back, closer than necessary, should he have to spot her. I've watched her though. Ari doesn't need a man. She's her own knight.

"Okay, you ready?" he laughs. His head dips, so their cheeks almost brush.

My fingers curl into tight fists at my side. The deep breaths I am attempting do nothing to calm the rage. My feet charging forward the moment his fingers wrap around her hip.

"I was born ready," she replies. There's no humor in her response, just stone-cold determination as her lips clamp tight with her grunt. She lifts the bar from the rack before her knees bend. Her ass curves out and I want nothing more than to palm it until she incidentally brushes Oliver's leg. My focus quickly reverting to plotting his murder.

Then she groans. My dick twitching in response. Her toned thighs quake as she sinks lower. The descent so slow it almost seems sexual. There's no amount of adjusting my solid erection in my shorts that will make me any more comfortable.

"Hey, man," a hand clamps on my shoulder as I spin to find Tuck and Bronson behind me. There are a few of the younger wolf shifters with them too, but I barely acknowledge their presence.

The *thunk* of the bar dropping onto the rack has my heart racing. Spinning on my heels, I zoom in on where Ari stands. It's not like I don't know she'll be fine. I just needed to see it for myself. Her hip cocks to the side, hands braced on them as she stares me down.

"Way to fuck with my focus," she snips.

Tuck's hands go high in a gesture of peace. "Sorry. Adrian doesn't work out here much. He hates us all interrupting the Zen of his workouts," Tuck chuckles, another clap thumped against my shoulder blade.

Those blue eyes find mine. Where they shone like sapphires in the setting sun, in the artificial light, they were as dark as the deepest oceans. A navy blue so rich it would be impossible not to get lost in them. If I ever did, I'd never find my way out.

"I come here all the time," I brush Tuck off. Averting my gaze for a few seconds so I can slip back into my asshole mask.

With each passing day, it's a greater challenge to play the brooding dick when it comes to her, but what choice do I have?

"A lot more since Ari has been here training. If you wanted to make sure she was getting proper instruction, you should have told Mom."

He claps me on the shoulder once more before sauntering off to the free weights. This is one disadvantage of being paranormals with short tempers and training regimens that resemble Navy Seals. Regular gyms make us stand out, so most of us come here. Hence, no escaping that woman that my soul calls to. Longs for.

I know Tuck means nothing by his comment. It's purely business even if he's using that teasing tone. I have told no one Ari is my Pair yet. Out of fear. Or awkwardness. Or just trying to pretend like anyone else but our leader's long-lost daughter is my fated mate. Something like this could only happen to me.

It's been hell. Tampering the possessive nature that comes with the Pair bond takes far too much energy and focus. She's a distraction I didn't need, but cannot walk away from.

I can't be here. Can't stand here trying to destroy my body while I watch Oliver touch her and her flirt back.

"Hey, Tuck!" I call.

"Yeah, what's up?"

"We have business at your house."

He only nods, knowing exactly what I am referring to. The containment chambers below his home that house hostages. For those requiring a specific type of questioning, Tuck is very fond of dishing out behind closed doors.

He claps hands with the guys before meeting me in the doorway. My feet turning to move out of the space that puts me too close to Ari when her hand wraps around my wrist. I don't have to look to know it's her. My body already knows her. I was made for her. No matter how much I try to fight it. The worst part is I would want her even without the bond, but my position and who she is drew the line we can't cross.

Yanking my arm from her, I turn the asshole back on, no matter how much it kills me to.

"Hands off."

She only rolls her eyes, her hands drifting to her hips. "We still on for tonight?"

Fuck. I shouldn't have promised I would look through her cases with her. She thought there might be other paranormals we could add to the list alongside my kill sheet.

I can't resist my pull to her as I step in closer. My head dipping so our noses nearly brush. Typical for us. I can sense her body heat with our proximity. Smell the arousal pooling between her legs. Legs I want to be nestled between. No doubt everyone is aware of what's happening here, but they're smart enough not to say anything.

"Can't stand a night away, huh?" I ask. My voice goes husky and low and, fuck, all I want to do is kiss her again. Just devour her mouth as I sink my cock into her soaked pussy.

Fuck.

I need to get out of here.

"Don't flatter yourself," she scoffs. "My place. Ten. Don't keep me waiting."

She eyes me once as she struts away from me. "Oh, and Adrian," she calls over her shoulder. "Bring me something good." Her smirk in place as she joins Oliver at the rear of the gym, plopping down onto the mats. I can only stand watching for a moment before I drag my gaze away. Jealousy and anger swirl inside me. *Chill, Adrian.*

"You better drive fast as hell," I warn Tuck.

"No problem," he claps my back again and we're gone.

It takes an hour to reach Tuck's house. A home similar to mine nestled in a suburban area of Chicago. We both needed space for our reasons, but also wanted to remain close to downtown.

The house is quiet as we enter. Even if our captives were shouting at the top of their lungs, the rooms are soundproof, with walls reinforced with dermanium—a metal alloy that can ultimately ruin any paranormal. For a phoenix, though, it's our death sentence.

"Who do we have tonight?" I grunt as we make our way down to the basement. One side of that door is a modern home. The moment you cross that threshold, it transforms into a dark concrete space. The entire basement, except a small storage room, is outfitted with these torture rooms. Ten by eight cells for us to use at will.

There are few occasions I have the stomach to witness this side of Tuck when he gets going, but since Ari barreled into my life, I've taken part.

"One of Salvatore's club operators. He was pretty tight-lipped when we brought him in, but I'm sure he'll loosen up if you're joining me."

In an instant, Tuck's expression changes. The sweet guy he is most of the time becomes overshadowed by the dark, menacing, and unhinged version of himself. The switch flipped so quickly it could give you whiplash.

He's never explained to me why he's like this and, frankly, it's not my business. But it's been damn helpful as of late.

"We'll make him talk quick, then. I only have three hours before I meet our girl." The words slip free so naturally. Tuck quirks a brow but says nothing. He knows I'm talking about Ari. We had an awkward conversation about the kiss. He just made me promise to either keep my hands to myself or do her right.

I lied.

Told him it was the heat of the moment and there was nothing more to it.

Funny, until the look he just gave me, I was certain he believed it. Convinced his flirtatious tone when he talked about Ari and me stemmed from our conversation over a month ago, when I told him she was following me.

Tuck shoves open a door at the end of the hall. A short but burly guy comes into view. His thick body sausaged into the spelled ropes holding him in the chair.

"Hi Zed," Tuck chuckles. "I brought a friend this time." One by one, his fingers shift into the talons of his Phoenix. Tuck has the most insane control I've ever seen when it comes to partially shifting. His preference when doling out his special brand of torture.

I allow my talons to form, too. My teeth become miniature knives in my mouth. The sharp points grazing along the inside of my lips. One false move and they'll pierce right through the flesh.

"Zed, what do you have to tell me?" I grin, each of those sharp points on display.

He spits at our feet. Tuck laughing maniacally as he slices his claws across the man's chest. His howl rings through the room as crimson blood blossoms along the slash lines. His pale cream button-down now destroyed.

"I'll ask again. What do you have to tell me?"

"Fuck. You," he spits. His breathing now ragged.

Blood oozes quicker than it should. A small pool forming on the chair between his spread thighs.

Lunging for him, I dig a talon straight into his left pec. Another howl released. My grin spreading knowing no one can hear him but us. Twisting, it sinks in deeper. I'd purposely picked this side, not quite ready to stop his heart.

"Okay. Okay. Please stop," he sobs. Drool trickles from the corner of his mouth tinged pink from likely biting his tongue or the inside of his cheek. "Salvatore knows about you and Ari. He knows and he's..." his voice trails off as his head lolls to the side.

Fucking hell. Humans try to crap out on us so quickly.

Tuck slices at him again. Zed waking with an ear-piercing scream. This set of claw marks deeper than the first.

"Finish what you were saying."

"Salvatore wants you dead, but he'll kill her first just because of what she means to you." The words labored as he pants them out between winces.

Tuck moves unnaturally quick, his body lining up behind Zed's. The tips of his talons rest at the man's temple, ready to puncture through tissue and bone if Zed doesn't give me the answer I want.

"Ari means nothing to me," I growl. It's a lie, but I'm not ready to broach this with Tuck yet.

Zed laughs. Whole, hardy, and loud as his head flies back, ignoring the sharp points at his temples.

"Biology says differently," he chortles.

I barely realize I've moved until I hear the snap of his neck. My hands pulling away from him the moment his body slumps forward.

Tuck only stares at me. "What was he talking about?"

"I have no idea."

Another lie.

But a new purpose.

Salvatore will have to go through me if he thinks I'm letting him murder my Pair.

Ari. Is. Mine.

Bonus Chapter 3

Adrian

I'm losing my mind. Positively, absolutely, losing my fucking mind.

It's been five days since I told Ari she's my Pair. She's been avoiding me since. When we're in the same room, her eyes dart in another direction. They move so quick I don't know how they stay put in her head. There's no bite to our interactions. None of the usual banter and spewed words. Not a single phone call, just one-word answer text messages.

It was no better when I arrived for dinner at the safe house last night. Ari all but ran from the house. Her goodbye to her brother and mother carelessly thrown over her shoulder. The roar of her Mustang's engine hitting us less than a minute later. I'd only received awkward stares and pitying looks from Syriah. It was the most unbearable two hours of my long life.

I can't stand it. Any of it.

But I don't know what I really expected. Her to jump into my arms and say, "Take me now." That's not Ari. That's not our dynamic at all. But maybe I would have at least thought she'd fight with me about it if nothing else.

After I'd killed Zed, I knew I needed to come clean to Tuck, and I did. I told Syriah, too. She only giggled in my face as if she already knew. I suspect maybe she did. Nothing gets past her. She'd hugged me close, whispering in my ear, "There's no one I would prefer to take care of my daughter than you."

I swore my fucking heart was going to explode. Syriah has been the mother mine never was. Loving. Supportive and always on my side. She has no idea what it meant to me for her to entrust her daughter to me. To my birth parents, I was never good enough. But to Syriah, Lanham, and everyone who stands with them, I've done so much right.

My eyes burn, remembering that moment. Wishing Lanham had been there, too. I would hope there would be joy behind his eyes. That he would see I'm nothing like my family and worthy of bonding with Ari.

I check my phone for what must be the millionth time in the past hour. Ari and I were supposed to meet tonight, but she hasn't answered me all day. Truthfully, the only thing that makes me feel better is knowing she works with her partner, a wolf-shifter, and Oliver has stayed clear of her except house business.

She's taken to training with Tuck. It would've been nice if she asked me, but why would she? I've treated her like shit for months and then dropped a bomb on her. And the way I kissed her. Like she was already mine. No wonder she wants nothing to do with me.

But she'd kissed me back. Pulled me closer even. Her mouth moved with mine as if I belonged to her, too. As if she wanted this bond sealed as much as I did.

No matter how much I crave her, even if she agreed that night, I wouldn't have taken things further. I need her to understand what it really means to bond with me. To someone like me. I need her to choose it with a clear picture in mind. Until I know she chooses me the way I already have her, I won't go there.

My mind does anyway. Imagining what it would be like to run my hands over her bare skin. Her toned body writhing beneath me as I sink into her tight cunt. Her walls squeezing tight, keeping me buried inside her.

"Fuck, Ari," I groan as my dick swells in my sweats. My pelvis flexes as I let my mind drift to her. My rough palm rubbing over where my thick length throbs. Heat permeating through the fabric searing my skin.

A clear vision of her floats across my mind. Those legs wrapped around my waist. That fucking smirk that makes me want to bend her over and fuck her against the kitchen island on display.

"Fuck!" I roar as my hands grip my hair. My eyes fly open.

I need to get a hold of myself.

Need to stop fantasizing about a woman who may never choose me.

Shoving off the couch, I stomp toward my bathroom. A cold shower will have to do.

I go through the motions. Short commands recited for each action.

Turn light on.

Step into shower.

Turn on water.

Wait.

Don't touch my dick.

Strip.

Relax into the water.

Except, I don't. I can't.

The moment my palm slides over my wet chest, I imagine it's hers. Those long fingers exploring my body. Nails scraping across my flesh as she takes what she wants.

"You like touching me, Ari?"

I can hear her hummed response. *"Maybe."*

My hand drifts down my torso. Crawling over my tightening abs before fisting my dick and pumping.

I keep the rhythm slow, drawing out this fantasy. This might be the only way I get to have her. I want it to last. I want her here with me. Her body soaked under the spray of the water as I explore her. My fingers sinking into her pussy, driving her to the edge. A tease before I slip inside her, fucking her until my name is the only one she knows.

My fist pumps faster. The exaggerated tug when my hand reaches my head making me groan louder each time.

"Yes, baby. Just like that. Take my cock."

My breath comes in heaving pants as I lean against the wall. The pads of my fingers finding little purchase as my abs flex.

"Fuck, Ari. You're mine."

"Yes." Her voice fills my head again.

I move faster still, my body on the verge of coming undone.

"Come with me, baby. Come all over my fucking dick."

The first jet of cum sprays my shower wall. My breath ragged bursts past my lips. More and more thick ropes spray every surface. My body vibrating with the intensity of my orgasm.

I've barely come down when I hear my phone ring on the bathroom counter.

Quickly removing one showerhead and spraying down the walls and floor, I throw a towel around me.

"Hello!" I pant, one hand resting on the counter.

My body is still wrecked from my release. My dick still semi-hard ready to continue its fantasy of her.

"Why are you breathing so hard?" Ari quips.

Fuck. My eyes press shut, praying she doesn't suspect what I was doing. My gaze drifts back to the shower, checking for the evidence as if I expect her to come in and inspect my bathroom tonight.

Then I feel it. Feel her. That tugging within, calling out to her. My Phoenix wants this bond the same as I do.

"Nothing. What's up?" I swallow, attempting to sound calm. But I can hear my ragged breathing as well as she can.

At least she's not here to see the flush covering my naked body.

She's quiet for a few moments. So quiet I pull the phone away from my ear, checking that the call didn't disconnect.

"I'm outside. Let me in."

Fuck!

Also by Britton Brinkley

Misfits Series (with L.A. Scott)
Misunderstood

Misfortune

Accepted

Night Life Duology
Night Life

Night Life 2: Will to Fight (10.25.24)

The Company Series
The Tournament

The Target (COMING SOON)

Disavowed Birthright Series
Rise of the Grisym

FEATHERS OF TRUTH

Dimmer of the Light (COMING SOON)

Fall of the Phoenix Series

Feathers of Truth

Feathers of Destruction (11.26.24)

Feathers of Change (COMING SOON)

About the Author

Britton Brinkley was born in New Jersey and now lives in Northern Virginia.

Growing up an avid reader, the sciences and ancient civilizations mesmerized her. She has always loved immersing herself in new worlds. Britton now enjoys creating her own with her writing buddies Jay Gatsby and the little psycho Artemis Prime (the cats).

When she isn't writing, she's likely either reading, watching Criminal Minds, or some other true crime show on Investigation Discovery.

Learn More at BrittonBrinkley.com

SNEAK A PEEK AT
BOOK 2 OF THE FALL
OF THE PHOENIX
SERIES...

Disclaimer

This is not a finalized version. Content is subject to change before the release of book 2.

Chapter 1

Ari

I've died once.

An excruciating tearing apart of my insides, burning them to ash before they could be welded back together. Before the bliss of rebirth filled my veins, elevating my being as if I was only the weight of the feathers my Phoenix bears.

An experience as terrifying as it was exhilarating. My first test of the limits of my mythological creature.

This death is no match. The burn never ends. My flesh continuously eaten away by the bullet lodged in the sinew of my chest.

I must be dead. Truly dead. Never to be reborn again. A Purgatory meant for those who have done wrong. Their indiscretions so unforgiveable no right could erase them.

There are no endorphins this time. No sweet release to settle the aches of my body breaking apart into the tiniest particles of being and then rebuilding.

Yet a voice reaches the outer edge of this consciousness. His voice. The deep timbre vibrating in the darkness above me.

Each word smothered in fear. Desperation dripping from every syllable. Pleas and bargains made that may go unanswered.

I'm dead.

I'm dead.

I shouldn't be able to feel his arms around me. Shouldn't be able to curl into the warmth of his breath on my face or the vibration of his chest against my spine.

I'm dead.

The pain is too much. Too intense for me to fight against. The intensity not worth the struggle to stay here with him.

I tried.

I came here to end Salvatore Danarius once and for all. An attempt at stopping him before he could dismantle both the human and paranormal worlds any further. Before he can rain down more destruction than we can feasibly recover from.

I tried.

I failed.

Forgive me, Adrian.

In time, my family will freely give that forgiveness. They'll understand I did what I did for all of us. The others will, too. But will Adrian? The man I unknowingly fell for. Will Adrian excuse me for sneaking out in the dead of night to save them all?

Deep down, I know the answer. *No.* He won't. And that knowledge shatters my heart even more painfully than the scorching burn working its way through me.

I was ready. My finger was already pressing against the trigger when he called my name. I finally admitted to myself that I couldn't live in a world without this man.

My name uttered on his lips is all it took. Just that split-second of hesitation was all it took for Sal to pull the trigger. My murder is likely a conundrum warring inside him. He killed his prized hitwoman — a loss that will sit with him — but likely felt nothing as he watched me crumple to the floor.

I am just a corpse now to Sal. Nothing for him to worry his pretty little head over anymore. For me, I linger in this place in between. Every morsel of pain felt as if I am suspended in time. The essence of Adrian keeping me just close enough to feel him. To hear him pleading for me not to leave him. To make it out of this. Come back to him.

I'm sorry, Adrian.

Adrian Alexander, the Second to my parents ruling over the creatures like us, does not beg. He is cold and brutal and unforgiving. He does not beg, but he is my Pair. My other half. A bond between us we didn't choose, but will keep us tethered together even if we never choose one another.

But I choose him with every fiber of my being.

Of course, I would decide such a thing after I'm dead.

Dying.

No, dead.

Whatever I am.

Fuck, it hurts. My insides scorched against the unique metal nugget that pierced my skin, nestled just above my heart. I can feel it there. Moving with each ever-slowing beat. The tiny shifts causing more damage than could be imagined.

I never understood what my bullets did to those like us until now.

I'm so, so sorry.

My strength weakens. Slower. Slower. Slower. Weaker. Nearly gone. My lungs ache. It's impossible to draw breath. To breathe in the man above me.

I am losing him.

I am losing my connection to this world.

The surrounding darkness becomes impossibly more inky. Nothing seen. Nothing heard. Nothing felt.

I can't fight anymore. I accepted the risk of coming here tonight. Of knowing it might be my last. I can only hope he'll let my already dead body release the soul that is still clinging to him and finish the job I couldn't.

I'm sorry, Adrian.

Made in the USA
Middletown, DE
19 April 2025